SIX-GUNS BLAZING

TWO NOVELLAS

ANDY RAUSCH

CONTENTS

WYATT EARP AND THE
DEVIL INCARNATE

Dedicated to the memory of my late friend Budd Boetticher, the best damn Western filmmaker of all time.
You are missed, my friend.

If this ain't the way it was, it's the way it should have been.
—John Milius, *The Life and Times of Judge Roy Bean*

ONE
A NIGHT AT THE ORIENTAL

I⟨T WAS⟩ a Saturday night like any other at the Oriental. The saloon was packed, overflowing with drifters, gunmen, gamblers, and the dregs of society. Red played a ditty on the old piano, barely audible over the din of drunken patrons. The smells of cigar smoke, sex, and body odor filled the place, giving it the same generic odor found in any saloon on a busy night.

Deputy Marshal Wyatt Earp was, as was usual on such a night, holding court over the faro table. His older brother, Virgil, the town marshal, was sitting to his right, downing his fair share of free whiskey and smoking Wyatt's cigars. To Wyatt's left sat notorious sporting man and cold-blooded killer Doc Holliday—Wyatt's only friend—smoking a cigar, downing glass after glass of high-end scotch, and making lewd remarks to anyone who might indulge him with a listen.

"It's a hell of a night tonight, Wyatt," said Doc.

"I don't like it."

Doc grinned. "You don't like anything."

"I got a bad feeling." Wyatt, being a lifelong lawman, was prone to such gut feelings, and they were seldom wrong. He almost always knew when trouble was about to jump off, seeming to somehow smell the tomfoolery in the air. And now his gut was telling him things could get ugly any minute.

He scanned the room, looking for potential problems. Doc was used to Wyatt's keen ability to sense such things, so he paid him no mind. Inebriated, he just kept on blabbing about the superiority of a Georgia gentleman over just about any other man created by God.

Watching a group of cowboys over Doc's shoulder, Wyatt engaged his friend. "If you love Georgia so much, why don't you go back there?"

Doc chuckled. "You know I can't go back there, Wyatt. I love the beautiful state of Georgia, but it turns out she does not share the same love for me."

"Problems seem to follow you everywhere you go," said Virgil.

Doc raised his glass. "That does seem to be the unfortunate truth."

Wyatt continued his inspection of the room, but saw nothing out of the ordinary.

This time—once in a million—he didn't spot the trouble because it was directly behind him. But Doc saw it clearly. A little whiny troglodyte of a brute named Ike Clanton was putting his arms around Doc's traveling mate and companion, Kate Elder, and she wasn't enjoying it one bit. Ike's hand slid up to grab a handful of Kate's sizeable bosom. She slapped him away, but still Ike persisted.

Doc stood, staring at Ike. He poured himself another drink, downed it, and said, "If you'll excuse me, fellas, I have pressing business to attend to." And Doc started walking towards Ike.

Virgil now saw what Doc had seen. "Aw, hell," he said.

Wyatt spun around in his chair to get a look, now seeing Ike putting his hands on Kate.

Doc approached Ike, but the damned fool didn't see him coming as he was too busy fondling Kate. When Ike saw Kate looking at Doc, he turned around and found himself face to face with Doc's nickel-plated .41 caliber Colt Thunderer.

Ike's eyes got big.

"I don't believe we've had the pleasure of introduction," said Doc. "My name is John Holliday."

Ike said nothing.

"And this woman you've been putting your grubby little paws all over is named Kate."

"I didn't mean nothin'," Ike said. "I was just foolin' around, having a good time."

Doc looked at Kate. "Then why doesn't *she* appear to be having a good time?"

"I didn't do nothin' wrong."

"Where I'm from, a man doesn't grab a lady's breast without her consent," said Doc.

"But she ain't no lady. She's a whore."

Doc cocked the pistol. "That may well be the case, but she's *my* whore."

Now members of Ike Clanton's gang were moving in to surround them. One of the men, a smart-assed cattle rustler named Curly Bill Brocius, drew his Colt .45 and put it to Doc's head. Only seconds later, Wyatt held his own Schofield Smith and Wesson to Curly Bill's head.

Doc grinned his big trademark shit-eating grin. "Well, I do believe we have us a party now. *Woo-wee!*"

Curly Bill growled, "Shut up."

Doc looked over at Wyatt. "How nice of you to join us, Wyatt."

Now Virgil jumped into the fray, waving his revolver around, telling everyone to put away their weapons. "Stop all this *now!*" he demanded, but no one moved so much as an inch.

"If you don't put down your pistol, sir, I will be obliged to shoot a big hole through your little friend," said Doc, his condescending tone an invitation to test him.

"And if you shoot him, then I shoot you," said Curly Bill.

"I guess this is the part where I'm supposed to say then I'll shoot you," said Wyatt.

"*Goddammit, Wyatt!*" said Virgil, losing his patience.

Curly Bill smiled, looking at Doc. "I believe it's your turn now."

"Aren't you a clever devil?" said Doc.

Tired of the bullshit, Wyatt smashed Curly Bill over the head with his revolver, knocking him to the floor unconscious.

Ike's eyes got big again. "You can't do that!"

"I believe he already did," said Doc.

Wyatt holstered his pistol. "Why don't you and your boys clear on out of here before there's *real* trouble...the kind you won't walk away from."

"What kind of talk is that for a lawman?" asked Ike. "That ain't right!"

"Let the man go," said Virgil.

As usual, no one listened to Virgil. Doc kept his gun pressed against Ike's temple.

"Come on," said Wyatt. "Put away the gun."

Doc holstered his weapon. "If you aren't the very voice of reason, Wyatt Earp."

"You boys ain't gonna get away with this," said Ike. "We'll be back."

Wyatt said, "Can't you see I'm trying to let you leave here alive? Are you really so stupid you can't see when it's the proper time to shut your damn fool mouth?"

Ike backed away, threatening, "You ain't heard the last of us, lawman."

But Doc just waved him away nonchalantly. "You may

leave now, sir. I believe our business here has reached its conclusion."

Ike elbowed one of his men, motioning for him to leave with him.

Virgil pointed at Curly Bill. "And take this no-good son of a bitch with you."

VIRGIL WAS PISSED. Wyatt was a natural-born lawman, and Virgil was, to his chagrin, somewhat lacking as a peacemaker. Virgil didn't get the respect he felt he deserved, and what little respect he did receive came from his being the brother of the famed Wyatt Earp, legendary lawman out of Kansas. Both Virgil and Wyatt knew the score. They both knew Virgil wasn't cut out to be the marshal, but neither of them had ever said a word about this before.

"How the hell am I supposed to maintain order here with you and Doc gallivanting around here as you please, acting like a couple of damned outlaws?" asked Virgil.

Doc said, "Hold your tongue, Virgil. I am still a proud card-carrying member of the outlaw club, and I have absolutely no desire to be a lawman of any kind."

"Well," said Virgil, "you've got an excuse. But you, Wyatt, you should know better."

"And what?" asked Wyatt. "Let them get the drop on Doc? Let them run wild and shoot up the place? Let them rape Kate?"

"I appreciate the sentiment, Wyatt, but I could have taken them both," said Doc.

"Not when you're drunk you couldn't have," said Wyatt.

Doc smiled. "My being drunk is the only reason I claimed possibility to shooting only the two of them and not their whole damned inbred band of misfits and miscreants."

Wyatt and Virgil ignored this, and Virgil went on saying his piece. "We're the law here, Wyatt. We—"

"There ain't no law here!" said Wyatt. "This isn't Wichita, where you can just play happy lawman and finesse your way out. This is Tombstone. It's a whole different game here. You have to stand up to them. You have to think on their level. You have to act on their level. If you don't, then they've already won the damn battle. So, if you want to act like you're their friend, then you go ahead and do it and I'll just keep coming along behind you and cleaning up the mess."

Virgil was visibly hurt. "That's not fair."

"Fair?" asked Wyatt. "Fair's got nothing to do with it. If you're looking for a fair fight, you need to go somewhere else, Virg."

Virgil started to stutter, but Wyatt cut him off.

"When Curly Bill and Clanton threw down, you just stood there like a stump," said Wyatt. "You don't have the instinct, and they can sense that. Do you think they can't? Hell, a blind man could see it a mile away."

Doc was the first to sit down. "Let's all have a drink or two and relax a little bit before feelings get injured and whatnot."

Wyatt and Virgil weren't ready to end their conversation, but Doc, who suffered from tuberculosis, started hacking up blood. Both of them saw this and decided to table the conversation for the time being. They looked at each other, exchanging a glance which said there would be a momentary truce. They sat down on both sides of Doc.

KATE APPROACHED THE TABLE. "You ready for bed yet?"

"*Ooh,*" purred Doc. "I do think I might get lucky tonight."

"Maybe," she said. "But only if you don't stay here too long."

"Honey, you read my mind," said Doc. "I do think I'll stay and have a couple more drinks with the boys here. Then I'll be home shortly thereafter."

Kate rolled her eyes but accepted it. "I'll keep the bed warm for you."

"That's not the only thing I want you to keep warm for me, Kate, my dear lady," said Doc.

Kate left and Doc returned his attention to the Earp brothers.

"I propose a toast," said Doc, raising his glass.

Virgil looked at him like he was crazy. "To what?"

"To new friends," said Doc. "Let us toast our new pals, Ike and Curly Bill."

Wyatt looked at Virgil, half-smiling. "Haven't you learned yet? Doc doesn't need a reason to drink. Living's excuse enough for him."

"Regrettably, this is a fact," admitted Doc. "I do fear that I am becoming somewhat of an alcoholic. I do hope it doesn't affect my girlish figure."

Virgil and Wyatt both laughed.

"If you were any skinnier, you'd be invisible," said Virgil.

"You think I'm skinny?" asked Doc, grinning. "At least that's one good thing I can say for this damnable consumption I have—I don't get fat."

Now Virgil got serious, looking his brother straight in the eyes. "I've got to ask you something, Wyatt."

Wyatt said, "Anything, Virg."

"You've been spending a lot of time with that Jewish girl. The dancer."

"Josie."

"Right. Are you two an item?"

Wyatt's cheeks went red with embarrassment. "What do you mean?"

Doc spoke up. "What he wants to know is whether or not you're having sexual intercourse with that pretty young lady."

"I'm a married man," said Wyatt. "I don't engage in that kind of activity. Not anymore."

"If you say so," said Virgil.

Doc spoke up. "If Wyatt says he's not having relations with that girl, then that's it. That's the way it is. He's a damned fool if he's not, but then nobody ever said he was the smartest fella around."

A smile touched Wyatt's lips. "You're right, nobody ever said that."

"Then let us drink," said Doc. "To willful ignorance."

Virgil said, "There he goes with another toast."

Doc was about to say something smart, but old Henry Neville came running up to the table, shaken and out of breath.

"What the hell's the matter, Henry?" asked Virgil.

Henry looked past Virgil to Wyatt. "I found a dead woman outside!"

Wyatt started to stand. "A dead woman?"

"I tripped over the body in the alleyway. I reached down and tried to wake her, but she was covered in blood!"

"Who was it?" asked Virgil.

"I couldn't see who it was. It was too dark."

"Show us, Henry," said Wyatt. "Show us the body."

TWO
THE GRISLY FATE OF ARLENE GATES

THE BODY HENRY NEVILLE found was that of Arlene Gates, a prostitute who worked at the Crystal Palace. Arlene had come from Nebraska with her late husband, Durwood Gates, in the hopes of striking a claim and getting rich. But Arlene never got rich. All she got was dead.

In all his years as a lawman, Wyatt had never seen such a murder as this. Hell, he'd never even *heard* of a murder like this. The killer had sliced Arlene's throat from one side to the other. Then he'd disemboweled her. And she was missing an ear.

"What the hell do you make of this?" asked Virgil, sitting behind his desk, fiddling with a pencil.

"I'll be damned if I know," said Wyatt. "It's the craziest thing I've ever seen."

Their little brother Morgan, also a Tombstone deputy marshal, asked, "Why do you suppose the killer took her ear?"

Doc said, "Perhaps the man just has a fetish for ears."

"A fetish for ears?" asked Virgil.

Doc smiled. "I have been known to nibble on a female's ear on one or two occasions."

"So, what do we know about the killer?" asked Morgan.

"I think it's safe to say we're dealing with one sick son of a bitch," said Doc.

Wyatt said, "I think we can all agree that that's a fair assessment."

"Doc Goodfellow said the killer was shorter than Arlene," said Virgil.

"How could he tell?" asked Morgan

"They can tell from the angle of the cuts," explained Doc. "Those cuts'll tell you a whole story if you know what to look for."

Wyatt said, "The coroner said the incisions were extremely skillful, like those a doctor would make."

"You figure the killer's done this before?" asked Morgan.

"Could be," said Wyatt, nodding his head. "Could be."

"You figure he's somebody with medical training?"

"I dunno. At this point it could be anybody killed Arlene."

"If it's a doctor, he shouldn't be too hard to track down," said Doc.

"What about you, Doc?" asked Morgan, grinning.

Doc laughed. "While it is true that I was once a man of medicine, I myself was a dentist."

"What does that mean?"

"It means there wasn't a lot of call for me to disembowel anybody in my line of work," said Doc. "Besides, how do we know we can trust Doc Goodfellow? Maybe it was him that killed Arlene."

"Coroner by day, killer by night?" asked Virgil.

Doc said, "No killer is a killer all the time."

"Yeah," said Virgil. "Just look at you."

Doc gave him a go-to-hell look but said nothing.

"What do we know about the blade that cut her—anything?" asked Wyatt.

Virgil said, "The coroner figured the killer would have had to use either a scalpel or a sharp razor to make incisions like those."

"Maybe the killer is a barber," suggested Morgan. "A barber would have a sharp razor."

"Anything is possible," Wyatt said.

"So, we now have the search for the killer narrowed down to barbers, doctors, and coroners," said Doc. "We should have the killer in custody in no time."

"We've never seen anything like this in Tombstone before," said Virgil. "So, if the killer has done this before, he may be new to town. Have you guys seen anyone new that stood out?"

"Fifty new people come to Tombstone every day," said Wyatt. "It's a boom town. Could be anybody."

Morgan said, "I did notice one person we might need to speak with."

"Who?" asked Wyatt.

"An Englishman named Eldrich Davies came in on the stagecoach the other day. He looked kind of shifty."

"What else?"

"He's a doctor," said Morgan.

"Well then, he just moved to the top of our list of suspects," said Virgil.

"A doctor," said Wyatt, mulling it over.

"And a no-good Brit on top of that," said Doc, snooping through a stack of wanted posters. "He *must* be our man."

"Who else might we be looking for?" asked Morgan.

"Maybe he's a butcher," said Virgil.

Doc smirked. "Obviously."

"I mean a real butcher—as in someone who cuts meat for a living."

"I hate to shoot down your theory, Virgil," said Doc. "But a butcher hacks away at his work and uses a very big knife—not a scalpel. He wouldn't likely be able to make such a smooth incision such as those on our dearly departed Arlene."

"Did you know Arlene?" asked Morgan.

"I have only carnal knowledge of the woman."

"What does that mean?"

Doc smiled. "It means I worked with her on more than a few occasions."

"You sampled her wares?" asked Wyatt.

"Exactly, Wyatt. I sampled her wares."

"What do you remember about her?"

Doc gazed past them. "Boy, she had a mouth that could—"

"Will you guys get serious here?" said Virgil. "We need to figure out who might have done this."

"Obviously, we know who we're looking for now," said Doc.

"How do you figure?"

"We just have to find a short barber with a medical degree who's new to town."

Morgan smiled. He couldn't help it—Doc always made him laugh. The man had a way with words that was unlike anything the young deputy marshal had ever heard before. "I think Doc has figured out this whole case," said Morgan.

Virgil did not smile.

"You figure the Clantons might have done this?" asked Morgan. "Maybe on their way out of town, to get back at Wyatt?"

"No, the coroner said the body had been there for at least two hours," said Virgil. "Besides, I don't figure the Clantons for it."

"Why?"

"The Clantons like to shoot their enemies in the back," said Doc. "They don't cut them up. Besides, they were all too drunk to make such perfect incisions."

"Maybe we ought to ask old Evelyn over at the Crystal

Palace about Arlene's recent customers," said Virgil. "That might tell us something. Maybe she'll know if Arlene has had any trouble lately."

"That is an excellent idea to be sure," said Doc. "A fine idea indeed."

And off they went to the Crystal Palace.

THE CRYSTAL PALACE was almost as dead as Arlene Gates, but this was a Sunday afternoon, so it was to be expected. Today only the bartender and the whores were there, and the place stunk of cheap French perfume.

"Business is kind of dead today," observed Wyatt.

Zed, the bartender, said, "You can say that again. We ain't had but a few customers all day. I figured for sure things woulda picked up after church got out, but not today. How are things down at the Oriental?"

Wyatt lit his cigar. "About the same. Couple of drifters at the bar, that's about it."

"What can I do for you boys?" asked Zed.

"I take it you heard about what happened to Arlene Gates?" asked Virgil.

Zed nodded. "I did indeed. Damned shame."

"Do you know if Arlene had any trouble with anyone?"

"No," Zed said, shaking his head. "Everyone loved Arlene."

"You can say that again," said Doc.

"She have any rough customers lately?"

"Not that I know of," said Zed, wiping a glass clean. "But then you'd have to ask Evelyn about that one. I wouldn't really know."

"She around?" asked Wyatt.

"Sure. Let me get her for you." Zed turned and looked upstairs, yelling out, *"Hey, Evelyn! You got visitors!"*

Evelyn, the Crystal Palace madam, appeared at the top of the stairs, smiling big. "Why hello, boys." Making her way down the stairs, she turned to Doc, saying, "Hello, Doc. I ain't seen you in a day or two."

Doc tipped the brim of his hat to her.

"Damn Doc," said Wyatt. "How much are you in here?"

"Hell," said Evelyn. "If old Doc was here anymore, we'd have to give him a job. I swear he's here more than I am, and I live here."

Doc said, "You know I think you may be right, Evelyn."

Evelyn looked at Wyatt. "So, I guess you boys are here to ask me about Arlene."

"Unfortunately, yes," said Virgil.

"Well, I don't know what to tell you fellas. She was a great girl. Everyone loved her. She was one of our biggest earners. She'll be missed. She didn't necessarily want to be a whore, turned to it after her husband died and left her broke... But the girl did her homework for the job, and she was a real fast learner."

Wyatt asked, "What kind of homework might one do to become a whore?"

"Well, she studied the hell out of that *Kama Sutra*," said Evelyn.

"And I can assure you she put every one of those moves to good use," Doc said. "The author would have been proud."

Virgil rolled his eyes.

Morgan chuckled.

"This ain't no laughing matter," said Virgil. "A woman is dead here."

"Chopped all to hell is what I heard," said Evelyn. "That true?"

"I'm afraid so."

"I heard they cut off all her fingers, all her toes, both of her tits, both ears, and poked out her eyes."

Virgil paused before saying, "That's somewhat of an exaggeration."

"That's good to hear," said Evelyn. "That poor girl never did nothin' to no one. She was the most innocent whore I've ever known."

"Innocent whore," said Doc. "Kind of an oxymoron, don't you think?"

"She have any rough customers lately?" asked Wyatt.

Evelyn thought for a moment, shaking her head. "Not that I can recall. Again, everybody loved her."

"Apparently someone didn't," said Doc, lighting his cigar.

"I hate to ask this, but did she sleep with any of those cowboys that ride with Ike Clanton and his boys?" asked Virgil.

"Ike Clanton?" she asked. "I'm not sure I know him."

"Real hairy little fella," said Wyatt. "Dumber than a box of hammers. Full of hot air. Rides with a horse's ass named Curly Bill."

"Oh, *him*," said Evelyn. "Sure, I know that loudmouth. He's a grubby little thing, that one."

Virgil asked, "You know if he slept with Arlene?"

"I don't think so. I don't recall any of those cowboys paying for whores when they were in here. They get them up there at the Oriental?"

"Damned if I know," said Wyatt.

Doc smiled. "I just assumed every man paid for whores."

"You assume wrong," said Wyatt. "Not *every* man."

Doc rolled his eyes. "I forgot, the reverend Wyatt Earp doesn't pay for sex. Why, he's a married man."

Evelyn smiled big. "Maybe he just ain't met the right whore."

"What are you implying?" asked Wyatt.

"Maybe I could be the one to change your mind."

Wyatt grinned. "I appreciate the offer. I truly do. But no thank you."

"Can you remember any of Arlene's recent customers?" asked Morgan.

"Just one."

"And who might that be?" asked Wyatt.

"Some fancy-pants Englishman. I think he said he was a doctor."

Wyatt and Virgil looked at one another.

"You remember his name?" asked Virgil.

"It was a weird Brit name as I recall..."

Wyatt asked, "Was it Eldrich Davies?"

Evelyn's face lit up with recognition. *"That's it,"* she said. "That's him. Eldrich Davies! He was the last paying customer to sleep with Arlene before she was murdered."

"It looks like we're going to see Dr. Eldrich Davies," said Wyatt.

THREE
MEETING THE GOOD DOCTOR

WYATT SENT MORGAN and Doc back to the jail house to hold down the fort. Then he and Virgil asked around about Dr. Eldrich Davies and learned he was staying in the Grand Hotel. Largely because most everyone had a general disdain for Englishmen, no one had anything good to say. "He looks shifty" and "there's something strange about him" were the two most frequent claims they heard from the people of Tombstone.

When they arrived at the Grand, Wyatt and Virgil questioned the hotel manager about Davies, but learned little beyond the fact that he was a good tipper, and that the manager didn't much trust him either.

They also found that the good doctor was out.

"I think he went to get a shave and a haircut," said the manager.

"Any idea where?"

"Old John Hays cuts hair right around the corner. You might try him."

The two men left and walked around the corner to John Hays' barber shop. There they found a peculiar-looking, bespectacled little man sitting in the barber's chair, getting a shave. The moment Wyatt laid eyes on him, he knew what everyone else meant—there was *something* off about him, but Wyatt couldn't quite put his finger on what it was.

But the damn guy gave him the creeps. He knew that much.

Wyatt's gut told him this was their killer.

"You Eldrich Davies?" asked Wyatt.

The doctor didn't look at all surprised or worried to see two men with badges standing before him. If anything, he looked annoyed.

"Yes? Something I can do for you?"

"We'd like to talk to you," said Wyatt.

"About?"

Virgil said, "About the death of Arlene Gates."

"I have no idea to whom you're referring," said Davies. "I have no idea who this Arlene Gates person is."

"That's not what we hear," said Wyatt.

"I just got into town three days ago. I don't know anyone here."

"Evelyn over at the Crystal Palace says otherwise."

Davies said, "Well then I'm afraid she's mistaken."

"You calling Evelyn a liar?" asked Virgil, defensive now.

Davies looked more perturbed than flustered. "I'm afraid I don't know this Evelyn person either."

"Then I guess you're gonna have to come down to the jail house with us," said Wyatt, grabbing Davies' arm brusquely. When Wyatt grabbed the doctor's arm, John Hays jumped, inadvertently cutting Davies' cheek.

Wyatt now had Davies up and out of the chair, his face still half-covered with shaving cream. Davies reached up to where he'd been cut and looked down at the dark blood on his hand.

"I'm bleeding," he said.

"What about me?" asked Hays. "This man hasn't paid me yet."

Wyatt nodded at Davies. "Pay the man his money."

"But he hasn't finished shaving me," Davies said.

Wyatt tugged on his arm. "Pay the man."

Davies unhappily reached into his pants pocket, producing a handful of change. He paid Hays five cents.

"The price is ten cents," said Hays.

"What are you talking about?" asked Davies, pointing at the wall. "The sign right there says five cents for a shave."

"But you bled all over my apron," explained Hays. "Now I'm gonna have to buy a new one."

"But you were the one who cut me!"

Virgil looked at Davies. "Kind of a feisty one, aren't you?"

"Pay the man his five cents," ordered Wyatt.

"This is most absurd," said Davies.

Nevertheless, he handed over the five cents to John Hays.

"My good man," Davies said to Wyatt. "Could you unhand me momentarily so that I might remove this apron?"

Wyatt released his grip on the doctor's arm and Davies took off the apron, tossing it into the barber's chair.

"This is ridiculous," Davies said, noticeably perturbed.

They started walking towards the door. Davies grabbed his bowler hat from a peg on the wall. Wyatt looked back at Hays and said, "Give my regards to the missus."

"And you say hello to Mattie for me."

"I'll do that," said Wyatt.

The three men stepped out of the barber shop into the sunlight. There was a slight breeze, but it was still fairly warm for mid-October.

Wyatt took off his hat and fanned himself with it as they walked.

"Can I get a cigar?" asked Virgil.

Wyatt made a face as he reached into his jacket pocket. "You make more money than me, Virgil. Why don't you ever buy your own damn cigars?"

"Cause Allie won't let me."

"But she'll let you bum them off me?" asked Wyatt.

"She says money's too tight right now for unneeded expenditures."

"Excuse me, but who is this Arlene person, and what does she have to do with me?" asked Davies.

Virgil put the cigar to his lips and chewed the tip off. He then lit the cigar.

"She's the dance hall girl got killed last night in an alleyway near the Crystal Palace," said Wyatt.

"And I'm supposed to know her?"

"That's the story," said Virgil.

Davies at least tried to look like he was wracking his brain to remember. "Oh," he said. "The whore."

"Yeah," said Wyatt. "One in the same."

"I didn't even know her name."

"Just keep walking," said Virgil. "We'll discuss this down at the jail house."

And on they walked.

When they reached the jail house, Wyatt shoved Davies down into a chair.

"This is quite irregular," said Davies. "I haven't done anything wrong."

"You're our number one suspect right now," Virgil informed him.

"But even a suspect has rights."

Wyatt reminded him, "We're the law here. We decide what rights you do and don't have in this town. So shut your goddamn mouth and just answer the questions unless you want more blood on your face than there already is."

The ever-proper Englishman showed an expression of disapproval. "Very well then."

Morgan walked out from the back room and looked Davies up and down, sizing him up.

"Where's Doc?" Wyatt asked.

"He went down to play cards at the Occidental."

Wyatt nodded with understanding.

"You think this is our guy?" Morgan asked Wyatt.

"I'm not sure yet."

"This all seems very improper," said Davies. "I don't think—"

That was when Wyatt slugged him in the jaw, knocking Davies' head to the side. Davies reached up and touched his lip, finding more blood, just as Wyatt had threatened.

"Now, will you shut your damn mouth?" asked Wyatt.

"This girl, the whore," said Davies. "How was she killed?"

"Someone—some very sick cocksucker—sliced her up pretty good," said Wyatt.

"And you believe I know something about it?"

Virgil spoke up. "It was almost surgical, like it was done with a scalpel."

Davies grinned big now.

"I'd wipe that smirk off your face unless you want me to hit you a few more times," said Wyatt. "It's disrespectful to the—"

"*Whore?*" asked Davies.

Wyatt slugged him again, almost knocking Davies' chair over. This time Davies did not wipe away the blood. He just grinned, blood in the crevices of his teeth.

"You have nothing on me," said Davies.

"What makes you say that?" asked Wyatt.

"Because I, sir, did not commit this heinous crime."

Virgil asked, "So you admit you were with Arlene the day she died?"

"I admit that I paid her for her services," said Davies. "No crime in that, is there?"

"No, there's not," said Wyatt.

"I was lonely," said Davies. "We didn't even have sex."

"Then what did you do?"

"We talked. Like civilized people."

Virgil asked, "What did you talk about?"

"Life. The normal things a man and woman talk about."

"You expect us to believe that?" asked Morgan.

"What?"

"That you paid Arlene to...*talk*?"

"Look," said Davies. "You can't prove anything, so would you please let me go?"

All three lawmen disliked Davies' choice of words. He didn't say he didn't do it—he just said they had no proof.

"I don't like you," said Wyatt.

"Frankly, sir, I don't care much for you either."

"Do you own a scalpel?" asked Virgil.

Davies smiled. "What in the hell is this?"

"Do you own a scalpel?" repeated Wyatt.

"Of course I own a scalpel. I'm a doctor."

"Did you murder Arlene Gates?"

"This is preposterous."

"Did you kill her?"

"No, I certainly did not."

"Where were you last night between, say, ten and one?"

"I was out."

"Doing what?" asked Virgil.

"I went for a walk, and I caught the burlesque show at the theatre," Davies said. "Ask around, I was there."

"At what time?" asked Wyatt.

"Ten."

Virgil asked, "You stayed for the whole show?"

"No, I left in the middle."

"Why?"

"Because I was bored, just as I am now."

"I'm sorry," said Wyatt. "Are we boring you?"

"Yes, I'm afraid you are," said Davies, obviously trying to anger them now.

Wyatt backhanded Davies across the mouth.

This time Davies didn't flinch. He just sat there and took it, stone-faced. The condescending smile never left his face.

"You're starting to piss me off," said Wyatt.

"Well, this should be fun."

"If you didn't kill Arlene," said Morgan, "then why are you grinning like a damn madman?"

"Because you amuse me."

"How so?" asked Wyatt.

"All Americans amuse me," said Davies. "You're all so arrogant and self-righteous, all the while having no idea what complete and utter dolts you are."

"Are you calling me and my brothers dolts?" asked Wyatt, getting angrier by the second.

"I'm calling your entire country a nation of dolts."

And the man just kept grinning.

"You think it's funny that a woman died here?" asked Virgil.

"Of course I don't. Life is a very sacred thing."

"Are you a religious man?"

Davies laughed. "Not in the slightest."

"Do you believe in god?" asked Wyatt.

"No, of course not. Only an idiot would believe such superstition."

"What kind of man doesn't believe in god?"

"A man of medicine," said Davies. "Do you know how many men I've saved and how many men have died in my hands? If they lived, they lived because of modern medicine and my own skill as a physician. If they died it was because I couldn't save them. No god had anything to do with any of it. It was all me."

"Are you comparing yourself to god?" asked Virgil.

"Every surgeon is a god in his way," said Davies. "We control life and death. We hold it all in our hands. And I assure you, gentlemen, that's the only true god you're ever going to find in this world."

"You mentioned having people die in your hands," said Wyatt.

"I didn't kill that woman."

"How do we know that?"

Davies smiled again. "I guess you'll just have to take my word for it."

AFTER HOURS of questioning intermingled with the occasional punch or slap from Wyatt, they got nowhere with Davies. He would not admit to having murdered Arlene Gates. He only smiled that creepy smile and taunted them, ever insinuating that there was more to his story than he was telling them.

Finally, they let him go on Virgil's orders, but he was told not to leave the city limits anytime soon.

"What the hell did you do that for?" asked Wyatt.

"What?" asked Virgil.

"Let him go. You know damned well he committed that murder."

"But we can't prove it. Until we turn up some sort of evidence, we've got nothing."

"You don't have what it takes to be a lawman," said Wyatt.

"Here we go again."

"What do you think I would have done had I been the marshal here today?"

"Probably beat the hell out of the man worse than you already did," said Virgil. "And you know what? You still wouldn't have gotten anywhere."

"We could have forced him to sign a confession," said Wyatt.

"And that's justice in your eyes?"

"Frontier justice," said Wyatt. "It's the only kind there is."

Before Virgil could respond, there was a knock on the door.

Morgan opened it, and there stood Fred Schoemehl, the editor of the *Epitaph*, the city newspaper.

"Hey Morgan," he said, still standing in the doorway. "I wondered if I could talk to you fellas about last night's murder."

"Come on in," said Virgil.

Wyatt smiled big. He had an idea.

"We got the whole story for you," he said.

"You do?" asked Fred.

"We sure do."

"Why are you helping me?" asked Fred, suspicious. "You boys are never this helpful."

"Get out your pad and your pencil," said Wyatt.

"Alright." Fred opened his bag and pulled out a pad and set to take notes.

Wyatt said, "You ready?"

"Yes, sir."

"Okay, write this name down: Dr. Eldrich Davies."

Fred looked up. "How do you spell that?"

FOUR
WYATT AND JOSEPHINE

WYATT EARP HAD NEVER BELIEVED in things like love at first sight. Such things were beliefs held by women and poets, and he had previously believed himself incapable of such things. So, when he invited Josephine Marcus—a woman that, if truth be told, caused his heart to flutter a bit—to a picnic in the woods, he did so with the utmost belief that this could be done in the name of platonic friendship. After all, Wyatt was a strong man who had shown tremendous ability in just about everything else, so surely, he could hold his urges at bay.

Or so he thought.

But here they were now, sitting on a blanket, eating sandwiches, and staring at one another, and Wyatt knew for the first time that he wanted this woman very badly. Josephine Marcus was a woman who could make a man reconsider his beliefs.

He didn't want to flirt with her, but he could feel himself doing so. Even when they weren't speaking, he was seducing her with his eyes. And she didn't mind. She was doing the same thing back.

"I've never met a woman like you before," he said.

She smiled. "There are no other women like me, Wyatt Earp."

"You're so free and full of life. That's refreshing."

"What do I care what others think of me? I have no time for such foolishness. I enjoy the company of men, and I like to have a good time. I say what I mean, and I mean what I say. Life is too short for anything less."

"What will your fiancé Johnny say about us sitting here together like this?" asked Wyatt.

"Johnny Behan has nothing to say about what I do any longer," she said.

"Why is that?"

"For starters, he's no longer my fiancé."

"Really?" he asked.

"Really. And second, Johnny Behan is a horse's ass."

"There's something we both agree on," said Wyatt, smiling.

"You don't like Johnny?"

"No, I don't. He's arrogant," Wyatt said. "But not in a self-confident way, but the exact opposite. He's a man who seems insecure about himself, so he acts like he has confidence. He's cocky. And we don't see eye to eye on anything at all."

"Nor do we," she said. "Besides that, he's a no-good liar and a cheater."

Wyatt said, "He doesn't strike me as a man who would be a good lover. He seems too effeminate for that."

"I assure you that he's no great lover."

"Then how'd he get a pretty thing like you?" asked Wyatt.

"We were traveling across the desert in a stagecoach. It was Apache territory. He and a man named Al accompanied us on the trip to keep watch and keep us safe from the Indians. That...*interested* me. Besides, he was just about the only man present, so he seemed like a catch at the time."

Wyatt laughed. "Maybe under those circumstances, but that'd be about it."

She now turned her gaze to Wyatt. "I'll bet you're a magnificent lover. Are you a good lover, Wyatt Earp?"

Wyatt blushed. "What kind of question is that?"

"It's an honest one. I really want to know."

"Well, I've never had any complaints," he managed.

"What about that woman you travel with, that Mattie? Does she have any complaints?"

"I don't really want to talk about her," Wyatt said.

"Is she your wife?"

"She carries my name and we've been together for a while, but she's not my wife."

"Hmmm," said Josephine. "That's a good thing."

"Why?"

"Because I'm now interested in *you*, Wyatt Earp."

"Please call me Wyatt, not Wyatt Earp."

"Okay, Wyatt," she said. "Tell me something about you that I don't know."

Wyatt could feel himself dropping his guard with her. There was something special about this woman; he wanted to know her, and he wanted her to know him, which was something new for Wyatt.

"I used to be a bouncer at a brothel up in Peoria," he said.

"When was that?"

"This was a long time ago. Me and my brother Morgan worked there together."

"Did you enjoy that line of work?"

"It was the time of my life. I didn't have to deal with all the trouble and worry that comes with being a lawman."

Josephine asked, "Did you have sex with the prostitutes?"

"I'll just say this: it was not a job without its merits."

She smiled. "I like you very much," she said.

"I like you, too. Tell me about yourself."

"I like to tell people I'm the daughter of a wealthy German merchant, but it isn't true," she said. "I'm not even German. I'm Prussian."

"You speak Prussian?"

She laughed. "No, Prussian isn't a language. They speak Yiddish and German there."

"Which do you speak?"

"Both," she said.

Wyatt was impressed. He'd never met a woman with such sophistication and intelligence before. She was unlike anything else Tombstone had to offer.

"How did you become a dancer?" he asked.

"By luck. My best friend Dora was a dancer, and she convinced me to join her. Now we're performing 'H.M.S. Pinafore' at the Bird Cage Theatre. You should come see the show sometime."

"I definitely will," said Wyatt. "I hear you're quite good in it."

"Where did you hear that?"

"People talk."

"So how did you become a lawman, Wyatt?"

"The job was open, and I took it. That's about all there is to say."

"How long have you been a lawman?"

"A long time now," he said. "I used to be the marshal in Wichita and later in Dodge City."

"I know," she said. "As you said, people talk. Besides, you're practically a legend."

"Well, like most legends, a lot of what people say about me isn't true," said Wyatt. "I like to hear the stories myself, and they are entertaining, but they build me up so that it's difficult for me to live up to people's expectations."

"I doubt that," she said. "Tell me more about yourself."

"My brother Virgil arrested me last year, if you can believe that," he said, laughing.

"Truly?"

"I'm afraid so."

"On what charges?"

"Being a drunken ass," Wyatt said. "I got drunk and started a fight over a card game. Virgil took me to jail until I sobered up, and then he slapped me with a $25 fine on top of it."

She laughed.

"I like your eyes," she said. "They're pretty. They change colors... Sometimes they're blue, and sometimes they look gray."

"I like your eyes, too," said Wyatt. The truth was he liked everything about this beautiful, curvaceous young woman.

"What else have you done for a living, Wyatt?"

"I used to be a professional gambler."

She made a face. "Gamblers are generally dishonest people. Are you a dishonest man?"

He grinned. "Define dishonest."

"You do make me laugh," she said.

"So where did you live before you came to Tombstone?"

She looked off through the trees. "My family lived in Manhattan. In New York. It was an area known as the Five Points. We were very poor. That's why I tell people that story about being from a wealthy family."

"So why aren't you telling *me* that story?"

She smiled and gazed into his eyes, making his heart feel funny again.

"There's something different about you, Wyatt," she said. "I feel comfortable with you. I feel like I can be myself, and I don't feel that way about anyone else. Certainly not any men."

Wyatt knew what she meant. He felt the exact same way about her.

"I believe I'm going to fall in love with you," said Josephine.

Wyatt didn't know what to say, so he said nothing.

"I'd like you to call me Sadie," she said.

"Why?"

"My middle name is Sarah, and everyone back home calls me Sadie." She paused, staring into his eyes. "Can I be your Sadie, Wyatt Earp?"

Without giving thought to what he was doing, he took her in his arms, and he kissed her, their tongues exploring one another's. It was a powerful kiss, and Wyatt never wanted it to end. But finally, it did.

She tried to regain her composure, wiping her lips.

"You're a fine kisser," she said.

"I told you, no complaints."

They kissed again. This time it was her who made the move. Wyatt did not try to stop her. He went with it, eventually pulling his mouth away to kiss her neck. His hand moved up the outside of her dress to her bosom. She lifted her head to the skies, and he kissed every part of her body his mouth came into contact with, his hand still rubbing at her bosom.

And they made love, right there on top of the picnic blanket, rolling over half-eaten sandwiches as they did.

And it was wonderful.

WHEN THEY WERE FINISHED, they lay naked on the picnic blanket, staring at the clouds passing by.

"Does your job ever cause you to be afraid?" she asked.

"Not really," he said. "But this new killing... This Arlene Gates murder. It's something different. I've never seen anything like it. And that man, Eldrich Davies, makes me nervous. I've seen a lot of faces in my time, and none of them made me feel uneasy the way his does. There's just something about him. I fear he's..." Wyatt couldn't find the words.

"The devil incarnate," Josephine said.

Wyatt stared at the skies. She was correct. The killer seemed to be the devil incarnate. It was as though this woman had searched inside his brain. She somehow already knew him well enough to finish his sentences. She was a remarkable woman, to be sure.

"Wyatt?" she asked. "Why do you think people do things like that?"

"I don't know. I've known a lot of men who were just plain mean—just meaner than all hell—and there was no good reason for it. Some men are just born bad, I guess."

"How about your friend Doc? Was he born bad?"

Wyatt smiled. "I wouldn't exactly call Doc 'bad.' He's more...misguided. That's the word I would use for him."

"Why are you friends with a man like Doc?"

"He's my only friend."

"I'm your friend, Wyatt."

"Thank you for that. I meant he's the only true male friend I have. He doesn't judge me, and I don't judge him."

"Is he a bad influence on you?" Josephine asked. "Or is it the other way around?"

"Depends on who you ask, I guess. Most people think he's a bad influence on me, but Big Nosed Kate thinks I'm the bad influence on Doc."

"Big Nosed Kate?" she asked.

"Kate Elder," said Wyatt. "She's Doc's woman."

Josephine was about to speak when they were interrupted by Morgan, riding up through the trees on horseback. Wyatt sat up, trying to cover himself. "What is it, Morgan?" he asked.

"Virgil needs you back in town," said Morgan.

"What's going on?"

"There's a mob out front of the jail house. They want to string up Eldrich Davies."

"Goddammit," Wyatt said.

His plan to involve the *Epitaph* didn't seem so clever at the moment. He wanted nothing more than to stay here in Josephine's arms and make love to her again.

But duty called.

Wyatt turned to Morgan. "You go on ahead. I'll be along directly."

He turned to Josephine, now covering herself with part of the blanket.

"I have to go," he told her. "Or else they're gonna kill that damned doctor."

"But isn't that a good thing?"

"Maybe," he said. Wyatt stood and put his clothes back on, tucking his shirt into his trousers. He put his holsters on, walked to his horse, and climbed on.

"I'll see you soon."

"Be careful," she said.

He turned back to her and said, "And yes, you can be my Sadie."

And he rode away.

FIVE
MOB MENTALITY

In the latest issue of the *Epitaph*, the good folks of Tombstone got to read all about how local law enforcement officers believed Dr. Eldrich Davies to be responsible for the grisly murder of dancehall girl Arlene Gates. The newspaper sensationally referred to Eldrich as "Doctor Death," further branding him as a murderer in the minds of the city's populace.

About an hour after the newspaper had been released, a drunken mob began organizing at the Occidental Saloon. It then carried down the street to the jail house, where Davies had already checked himself in for fear of death at the hands of vigilantes. Virgil was holding the doctor behind bars in protective custody. After the mob had arrived in front of the jail house demanding he hand Davies over to them, Virgil had gone outside, sawed-off 12-gauge Greener in hand, to try and quell them.

But talking had done no good thus far, and until Morgan and Wyatt got back, it was just he and Doc Holliday.

Virgil stood on the steps of the jail house, holding up the

shotgun where everyone could see it. Doc was behind him, leaning casually against the wall. As usual, Doc looked completely at ease in the situation aside from the occasional coughing fit. He was holding his own sawed-off 10-gauge Meteor.

It was big E.B. Thompson out in front of the mob, whipping them into a frenzy.

"E.B., why don't you take these people back where you came from," said Virgil. "No one's gonna take Eldrich Davies away from here today."

"Is it true he killed that whore?" asked E.B.

"I can only say that he's our number one suspect at the moment. It has yet to be determined whether Dr. Davies raised a hand against Arlene Gates."

"He gonna hang for what he done?" asked someone in the crowd.

Someone else yelled out, *"Bring out Doctor Death!"*

And soon the crowd was just as raucous as it had been in the beginning. Lucky for Virgil and Doc, Wyatt and Morgan were approaching.

E.B. Thompson looked over at them. "Wyatt ain't gonna stop us. Hell, it was him that said Davies was the damn murderer in the first place. I read it in the newspaper!"

Wyatt fired his pistol into the air, causing everyone to stop what they were doing.

"All of you had better disperse now," said Wyatt.

"And if we don't?" asked E.B.

"Then you can hang up there at that gallows with Davies," said Morgan.

This only made the crowd louder. Most of the members of the mob were already drunk at four in the afternoon, and by God they wanted Eldrich Davies dead.

"*Bring out Doctor Death!*" yelled someone, and it soon became a steady chant.

"I've said what I have to say," said Virgil. "We're going back inside now. If any of you sons of bitches tries to attack the jail house, you're gonna get a one-way ticket up to Boot Hill. I'm not in the mood for anymore of this bullshit!"

But still the crowd persisted chanting and screaming out threats.

"We're gonna get you Earps!" someone yelled.

Wyatt, now off his horse, waded through the crowd in search of the voice. "Who the hell said that?" he asked. But no one offered up the offender. Finally, Wyatt walked up the steps and followed Doc and his brothers inside the jail house.

They had been inside the jail house for several hours when someone threw a large stone through the window. There was a note attached to it, threatening that Davies would be burned out of the building if the Earps didn't hand him over to them.

Wyatt walked over to the window and yelled out, "You stupid sons of bitches! Do you have any idea how much one of these windows costs?" He paused, considered what he was saying, and added, "If anyone else comes up these steps, he dies. End of story."

Wyatt walked back to the jail where Davies was standing behind bars.

"The crowd's getting wild out there," Wyatt said.

"Why did you do this to me?" asked Davies. "This never would have happened if you hadn't planted that story in the newspaper."

"I wanted to draw you out."

Davies asked, "And?"

"Here you are," said Wyatt solemnly. "You know, you could make this all a whole lot easier if you'd just confess to what you did to that dancehall girl."

"I did nothing to anyone. Besides, what would confessing do? Speed up my death? Thanks to you I'm liable to die now no matter what happens."

"Then confess."

"You are, as they say, barking up the wrong tree," said Davies, still as calm and collected as ever. "I did not do a thing to that woman. As I said, we only had polite conversation."

"What if I was to go over to your hotel room and take a look at your scalpels? What would I find?"

"You are certainly welcome to do so," Davies said. "They are completely cleaned and sanitized. You will not find so much as a trace of blood on them."

"So, you admit that you did it?" asked Wyatt.

"I said nothing of the sort."

Davies' arms were folded around the bars. Wyatt grabbed them and yanked them forward, pulling Davies' face into the bars. *"You confess to what you did, goddamn you!"*

"I shall do no such thing."

Wyatt turned and looked at the broken window, seeing faces in the street outside. "What if I was to let you go?" Wyatt asked. "What would you think of that, Mr. Fancy Pants? What if I was to release you to that crowd and let them do what they wanted to you? Do you think your treatment would be better or worse out there?"

"My guess is about the same," replied Davies. "You and the members of that mob share the same mentality, Mr. Earp. You need to look at yourself in the mirror and ask yourself if you're a vigilante or a constable—are you good or are you bad?"

Wyatt spit in Davies' face, but the doctor remained unflustered. The spit dangled from Davies' moustache for a moment before the doctor wiped his face with the sleeve of his jacket.

THE MOB HAD DWINDLED a bit by sundown, and those remaining soon began carrying torches. E.B. Thompson had given up and gone home for supper, leaving the unruly mob without a central instigator. Just after dark, the crowd began screaming epithets and threats at the jail house again.

Soon a knock came at the door, and all the Earps drew their revolvers and raised them. The door opened, and all of them were prepared to shoot down whoever walked through it. Much to their surprise, it was Fred Schoemehl from the newspaper.

"Get inside and close that door," ordered Wyatt.

Fred did as he was told.

"You kind of got us at a bad time," said Morgan. "Can't you see we're busy here?"

"Well, I wondered if I could get the doctor's story in his own words," said Fred. "You know, before they break in here and kill him."

"Now why would I allow you to tell my story?" asked Davies through the bars. "You're part of the reason I'm in this predicament. You called me Doctor Death, for god's sake!"

Virgil spoke up. "Don't you take my god's name in vain. You don't believe in god, remember?"

"I'll bet he's changed his tune on that one," said Wyatt, chuckling.

"And why would you presume such a thing?" asked Davies, haughty as ever.

"Most people in your situation would be crying and begging to the Lord by now. You mean to tell me you still don't believe in god?"

Davies sneered. "You tell me—where is your god today? Is he here with me, protecting me?"

"That's our job," said Morgan.

Davies laughed. "Exactly my point. I'm in just as much danger in here as I am out there."

"Between you and I," said Doc, "I don't much believe in god either. But then I'm just a scurrilous no-good scoundrel and a heathen, so nobody much cares about what I believe in."

IT WAS JUST after nine when someone tossed a lit torch through the window, catching the wooden jail house floor on fire.

"*Goddammit!*" screamed Wyatt. "You boys go in the back and get some buckets of water and attend to this. I'll take care of these limp dick sons of bitches right here and now."

"Well," said Doc. "I do believe I'll join you. I do always love to watch Wyatt at work."

Davies reached out through the bars, screaming. "*What about me? I'll burn in here!*"

But everyone ignored him, leaving him locked inside the cell.

Wyatt and Doc stepped outside, and a hush fell over the crowd.

Wyatt was now carrying Virgil's rifle. He held it up and fired it into the sky.

"All this bullshit stops now!" he cried out. "I'm gonna count to five, and any chicken shit still standing here when I get to five is gonna get a bullet through his heart!"

"One," he said.

Everyone in the crowd looked around nervously, trying to decide what to do.

"Two."

A few members of the mob broke away and left the crowd. "Three."

Now the crowd parted, and Curly Bill Brocius stepped out, his hand on his fancy two-gun rig. "Four," he said, catching Wyatt off-guard.

"What are you doing here?" asked Wyatt angrily.

"I hear you've got a murderer in there," said Curly Bill.

"Well," said Doc, "I'm sure you'd know all about that."

Curly Bill grinned, his hand now tickling the handle of his pistol.

"Let's have it out here, me and you, Holliday," said Curly Bill.

"I hardly think this is the appropriate time or place," said Doc.

"What are you, yellow?"

Doc was grinning now. "As much as I would so very much like to shoot you down dead in the street tonight, this is not an appropriate time or place."

"We've got business here," said Wyatt.

"I've got my own business," said Curly Bill.

"Oh, alright," said Doc. "If you really want to die tonight, I guess I could accommodate you." Now he had his handle on his own ivory-handled revolver, his eyes locked on Curly Bill's.

The moment was tense.

No one said a word.

Both men had their hands on their pistols.

Finally, just a moment before one of them would have drawn and killed the other, Wyatt reached out and smashed Curly Bill over the head with the butt of his rifle, once again rendering him unconscious.

"I do believe you've gotten quite good at that," said Doc.

"Now everybody go home, or you'll end up in jail here with Curly Bill!"

The remaining members of the crowd looked about one another, confused, and slowly started to dissipate. Soon there was no one left of the mob to threaten the Earps or to make demands. The street was completely empty.

SIX

THE BURDEN OF PROOF

THE EARP BROTHERS slept overnight in the jail house to ensure Davies' safety. Doc left to go play cards and "do some fornicating."

Bright and early the next morning, Ike Clanton and a few of his cowboys came riding in for Curly Bill. As was generally the case, Ike was in a foul-tempered mood. Having already knocked and been allowed into the jail house, he inquired about Curly Bill's situation.

Wyatt answered, "Curly Bill was arrested for inciting violence and threatening a lawman."

"I don't suppose you threatened him first," said Curly Bill.

"No, I don't reckon I did."

Ike tilted his head sideways and squinted at Wyatt, trying his damnedest to look tough. It didn't work. "What's the fine for that?" he asked.

"Thirty dollars," said Virgil.

"Well, I ain't payin' no damn $30 to get Curly Bill out of jail!" Ike proclaimed.

"Then it looks like he'll be staying with us," said Wyatt.

Ike looked over at Curly Bill, standing there behind bars in the cell next to Davies'. "Ain't you got some money?" Ike asked him.

"Nah, I ain't got no money," said Curly Bill. "Wyatt saw to that."

This irritated Ike, looking back at Wyatt now. "You took that man's money?"

"I unburdened him of it," said Wyatt. "Extra fines and whatnot."

Ike turned to Curly Bill. "How much did this sumbitch take off ya, Bill?"

"I had a roll," Curly Bill said. "Must have been two hundred if there was a dollar."

Ike looked back at Wyatt, who was grinning.

"What the hell kind of lawman are you?" asked Ike.

"The kind with $200," said Wyatt. "Now are you gonna pay the $30 to have Curly Bill here released or what?"

Ike mulled it over in his head, searching for something smart to say. When he couldn't come up with anything, he looked over at Davies, also standing there behind bars. "That there, that the man killed the whore?" asked Ike. "You're Doctor Death?"

Wyatt allowed Davies to answer for himself.

"You know how things tend to get blown out of proportion in this town," said Davies.

Ike nodded, looking back at Curly Bill. "Don't I know it."

Wyatt looked over at Davies now. "You and old Ike here would get along swell, Davies. I think you'd find that you share a lot of the same interests."

Ike glared at Wyatt. "What the hell is that supposed to mean?"

"It means you both enjoy killing people," Virgil said. "He cuts 'em all to hell, and you shoot 'em in the back."

"Maybe you should talk some more of your shit," Wyatt advised Ike. "Then you could stay here with Davies and you two could have a gay old time talking about all the criminal tomfoolery you've both been up to."

Ike was pissed. He took off his hat and shook it at Wyatt. "I don't appreciate your talkin' to me like that."

"Too close to the truth for comfort?" asked Morgan, lighting a cigar.

"Now are you gonna pay to take this miserable bastard Bill with you or not?" asked Wyatt.

Seeing there was nothing else to do, Ike reached into his pocket for his money. He counted out $30 and handed it to Wyatt. "I'd like a receipt," he said.

"Well, you ain't gettin' one," said Wyatt. "Besides, you and I both know you couldn't read it if I did give it to you. Now take this sorry son of a whore and get the hell out of my jail house."

Virgil unlocked Curly Bill's cell and let the man go free.

"We'll talk again," promised Curly Bill.

"One of these days you and I are gonna have one too many of these talks," said Wyatt.

"Meaning?"

"Meaning if Doc don't shoot you down then I might have to," said Wyatt. "Now both of you take your men and go home. I'm sure you got some cattle to steal or some square head to bushwhack somewhere."

Curly Bill just smiled, hat in hand, and headed for the door.

"We'll be back," said Ike. "Oh yeah, you goddamn Earps. We'll be back."

"Don't let the door hit you in the ass on your way out," said Morgan.

Curly Bill and Ike sauntered out through the doorway, trying to look tough.

"Good riddance," said Virgil, closing the door.

And that was that.

WYATT SAT THERE on Virgil's desk, staring at Davies. And Davies sat there in his cell looking at Wyatt. Each man studied his adversary, wondering just what it was that made him tick.

"When did you become a doctor?" asked Wyatt.

"Fifteen years ago," said Davies.

"What kind of medicine you practice?"

"I'm a general practitioner and a surgeon."

"What brings you to Tombstone?"

"Same as anyone else, I suppose," said Davies. "I came searching for prosperity. Besides, I heard they were short on doctors out in these parts. I thought maybe I could help."

"Yeah, you helped alright," said Wyatt dryly.

Davies stared at him. "Why do you take such delight in my misery, Mr. Earp?"

"Because I think you murdered that girl, and I'm not gonna be happy until I see you hang for it."

"Believe what you will, sir," said Davies.

"I will and I do," said Wyatt. "So, answer me this—when did you kill your first victim?"

"1864."

"You admit to killing someone in 1864?"

Davies grinned. "I killed a few people that year."

"How did you do it?" asked Wyatt.

"With a rifle, just like everyone else involved in the war."

Wyatt straightened. "You fought in the Civil War?"

"I did."

"But you're an Englishman."

"I *was* an Englishman," corrected Davies. "Now I'm an American citizen, just like you."

"Which side did you fight on?"

"Why, the Union side, of course."

Wyatt nodded. His brothers had all fought for the Union side, as well.

"I respect that," said Wyatt. "But what made you turn to crime—to killin' folks and such? Did something happen to you during the war?"

Davies laughed. "Do you really expect me to answer that?"

"You should. It would help your cause."

"Were I to tell you that I killed someone, I'd be dead within twenty-four hours."

"That's true, but you could at least die with a clear conscience."

"My conscience is clear, sir."

Wyatt tried a different approach. "Are you talented with a scalpel?"

"I'm a surgeon, for god's sake."

"There you go invokin' the name of my god again," said Wyatt. "Do it again and I'll punch you in your smart limey face."

"What, *again*?" asked Davies, trying his hardest to be a smartass.

"You just keep talking, Mr. Fancy Pants. You're gonna get yours. One way or the other, I'll see to it that you get yours."

"That much I'm sure of," said Davies.

Two DAYS later Wyatt and Virgil were sitting in the Oriental, eating bowls of rice with chopsticks, and sharing a bottle of Whiskey.

"It doesn't look like we're gonna get Eldrich Davies to confess," said Virgil. "Any ideas?"

"I've already knocked the hell out of him more times than I

care to remember, and he won't say nothin'," said Wyatt. "If it were me who was marshal, I'd torture him and force him to sign that goddamn confession."

"That's not my way."

"I know," said Wyatt, leaving it there.

But Virgil wanted to speak his piece. "I didn't get into law to coerce people into signing confessions that wasn't true. I got into law to help people, and that ain't helping people, Wyatt. What if that man's innocent?"

"What if he's not?"

"That very well may be the case," said Virgil. "But right is right and wrong is wrong. There's no gray area here."

Wyatt was already turning red. "Tell me you don't think he's our man."

"I do," said Virgil. "I absolutely do. But we ain't got proof."

"But what does your gut tell you? You're a lawman, same as I am, so you know by now sometimes you just gotta trust your gut instinct."

"You already know what my gut says."

"Then make him sign that goddamn confession and send him up to Wells Spicer so he can swing for what he done," said Wyatt.

Virgil slammed his fist down on the table, angry now. "I know you think I'm weak, Wyatt, but I'm not. I'm just a better man than you are. I know what's right, and that ain't right."

"But if you let him go and let him out there on the streets, he could do this again," said Wyatt. "He could do it to another dancehall girl. He could do it to anyone... He could cut up Allie, Virgil."

"I've said all I got to say on this topic," said Virgil.

Wyatt took a drink of his whiskey and said flatly, "Virgil, you're wrong. You *are* weak. You're the weakest man I've ever known, and one of these days it's gonna get you killed. Hell, it might even get us both killed."

Virgil took offense at this. "Say that again."

Wyatt calmly poured himself another glass of whiskey and downed it. He looked up, staring his brother right in the eyes and said, "You're weak, Virgil."

Within seconds Virgil was up and shoving Wyatt back in his chair. After almost toppling backwards, Wyatt leapt to his feet and slugged his brother. Virgil delivered an uppercut to Wyatt and soon both men were rolling around on the floor, knocking over tables and set on beating the hell out of one another.

WHEN WYATT and Virgil walked back into the jail house, they were bloodied, black and blue just like Eldrich Davies.

"What in god's name happened to you two?" asked Morgan.

"Why don't you ask your brother Virgil," said Wyatt.

Morgan looked at Virgil. "What's he talking about?"

"We're letting Davies go," said Virgil. "We got no proof of what he did, and we can't hold him here."

Davies, who was sitting in his cell, now stood up and walked to the bars.

"What the hell are you saying, Virgil?" asked Morgan.

"He's saying he's releasing that killer back onto the streets of Tombstone," said Wyatt. "Ain't that right, Virg?"

Virgil said nothing. He just picked up the keys to the cells and walked over to unlock Davies'.

"Thank you, Marshal," said Davies.

"Don't thank me," said Virgil. "It was the law saved you. I got no proof. I can't hold you here. Hell, I can't even tell you to leave town. But if you stay, you make sure you stay out of my way, Davies. Because so help me God, I see you in front of me again, I won't be so kind next time."

Davies said, "I understand, Marshal."

"One more thing," said Virgil.

"Yeah?"

"I better not find any more sliced up whores."

And with that, Dr. Eldrich Davies walked out of the jail house a free man.

SEVEN

A BAD DAY IN TOMBSTONE

When Wyatt walked into the Oriental the next morning, Ned the bartender was waiting to talk with him. "It's Ike Clanton," he said. "He's talking a whole lot of shit. He's saying he's gonna gun down the Earps and Doc Holliday. He's saying it's gonna happen soon."

"That's what men like Ike Clanton do," said Wyatt. "They talk."

"He's always in here shooting off his mouth about this and that, but this time it was different. This time it felt like he meant it."

"How long was he in here?"

"Couple hours," said Ned. "I think he was trying to drink up the courage to confront you boys."

Wyatt thought about it, pissed. "What else did he say?"

"He talked about having your wives murdered. He even mentioned your friend, the Jewish dancer."

"Josephine?" asked Wyatt.

"Yeah, her," said Ned.

Now Wyatt was good and angry. It was one thing to

threaten his brothers and friends, and it was another thing to make threats towards their wives.

Towards Josephine.

"I'll take a bottle of whiskey," said Wyatt.

"Are you sure that's a good idea?"

"Just give me the damned bottle," Wyatt said. "I'll decide what's good and what's bad for me."

Ned didn't say another word. He just got the bottle and handed it over to Wyatt, now sitting on a barstool. Wyatt took out a cigar, bit off the tip, and went to lighting it. He sat and considered all that Ike Clanton had said, drinking and becoming angrier and angrier by the second.

Finally, when his anger could rise no further and the bottle was empty, Wyatt stood. He briefly considered going after his brothers and Doc, but then thought the better of it. This was something he could handle by himself.

"Ike didn't happen to mention where he was going next, did he?" asked Wyatt.

Ned stopped wiping glasses for a moment. "You gonna kill him, Wyatt?"

"Where'd he go?"

"He said he was heading down to the Hatch Saloon to have a few more drinks and run his mouth a little more," said Ned. "What are you gonna do, Wyatt?"

Wyatt just turned and walked away.

It took Wyatt several minutes to get to the Hatch Saloon, which was down around the corner on Allen Street. Now he was liquored up and feeling invincible. He was ready for whatever Ike Clanton and his boys had to throw at him. He walked up the steps to the Hatch and threw open the doors.

He looked around the saloon and saw Ike at once. Ike was

sitting there alone at the bar, talking to the bartender. As Wyatt walked closer to him, he could now hear Ike spouting off the same horseshit he'd said back at the Oriental. "This time it's different," said Ike. "This time we're gonna gun those goddamn Earps down in the street in cold blood." The bartender looked up and saw Wyatt approaching, but said nothing. Ike just kept going. "And that damned Doc Holliday, he's the worst of 'em. Even that whore he runs around with is gonna get it."

Wyatt, now standing directly behind Ike, said, "Is that what you're gonna do, Ike? You're gonna murder my brothers and I? You're gonna shoot my friend John Holliday?" He paused for a moment before adding, *"You're gonna murder my friend Josephine Marcus?"* And he slugged Ike—*hard.* Ike fell back against the bar, bounced off and toppled to the floor.

The bartender threw up his hands. "I don't want no trouble in here."

"You should really watch who you serve in this place," said Wyatt. "You shouldn't allow patrons like this no-good pig-fucker in here. It's bad for business."

Ike was crawling around on the ground, trying to figure out what had just happened. Wyatt kicked him in the ribs.

"Say some more shit about me and my family," Wyatt said. "Go on, Ike, tell me all about your plans to murder us in cold blood."

Ike scooted his body back towards the stool.

"I didn't mean nothing," Ike was saying. "I was just talking. I didn't mean no harm."

And Wyatt knew then what he had always known—that a coward would say anything to save his ass.

But this time it wasn't enough.

He kicked Ike in the ribs again, and Ike crumpled under his boot.

"I'm sorry," Ike said, whimpering and starting to cry.

"You're right," said Wyatt. "You *are* sorry. You're a sorry sack of shit."

And Wyatt kicked him again.

And again.

And again.

ONCE WYATT WAS FINISHED KICKING the hell out of Ike Clanton, he sat down in Ike's stool, shadowing over the man on the floor. He ordered another bottle. Then he sat there and drank glass after glass, leaving Ike lying there in his own blood, still in possession of his revolver.

"Shouldn't you take away his gun?" asked the bartender.

"Nah," said Wyatt. "The man's too much of a coward to try anything. All he's good for is talk."

And Wyatt kept right on drinking.

He'd been doing this for some time when Morgan came looking for him.

Morgan walked up behind him, smoking a cigar. Wyatt could see his brother's reflection in the mirror behind the bar.

"What is it?" asked Wyatt, not turning around. "Can't a man drink in peace?"

Morgan looked down at Ike, lying there unconscious on the floor.

"Had another run-in with Ike Clanton, did you?" asked Morgan.

"You could say that."

"We need you, Wyatt."

Wyatt turned to look at his brother. "What's the matter?"

"There's been another murder," said Morgan.

"What kind of murder?"

Morgan shook his head. "Another whore. I'm afraid it's just like the Arlene Gates murder."

"No fooling?"

"No fooling," said Morgan. "She's cut all to hell."

"Where was the body found?"

"In an alley over by Sixth Street."

"You identify the body yet?"

"All we know is she's a whore," said Morgan. "No idea who she is."

Wyatt Earp finished his glass of whiskey and stood up. He turned, stepped over Ike Clanton, and headed for the door.

This was shaping up to be one hell of a bad day.

THE BODY BELONGED to one Mary Beth Shaffer, a Stover's whore out of Maricopa. Like Arlene Gates before her, Mary Beth had wound up alone in Tombstone, destitute and without family. So, she did what many other women before her had done—she turned to prostitution to make her way. Little did she know it would lead to her demise.

Mary Beth's body was lying crumpled between a couple of barrels and had gone unseen by passersby for a number of hours in the daylight before she was discovered by a drifter out of Missouri named Sutton.

"I was looking for a place in the shade to lie down and take a nap," Sutton had said. "So, I lay down, and looked over, and there she was, her dead eyes staring back at me. I damn near pissed myself right there."

Now Wyatt, Virgil, and Morgan were standing there in the alleyway, the barrels moved out of the way so they could get a good look at the body. Mary Beth was fully dressed, just as Arlene Gates had been, and she'd been sliced up. Her throat had been slashed, she'd been disemboweled, and one of her ears was missing.

"Where in the hell does he keep the ears?" Virgil asked.

"I dunno," said Wyatt. "Damnedest thing I ever saw."
Morgan agreed.

"I wonder what it is he does with them," said Virgil. "What he needs with them."

"Could be anything," said Wyatt. "Crazy son of a bitch like that, who knows what he's thinking?"

A few minutes later Doc Goodfellow arrived on the scene and looked over the body. "She's definitely been dead since sometime last night," he said. "And the incisions look almost identical to those of Arlene Gates. This was definitely the work of the same person."

Wyatt and Virgil then walked to Stover's to talk with Mary Beth's boss, Gilbert Riley. Riley was a middle-aged man who'd come out of Nebraska and had made a name (and a sizeable bankroll) for himself in dry goods. Once he'd raised enough money, he then bought out Jack Stover's brothel.

"Mary Beth's dead?" Riley asked, more than a little disinterested.

"I'm afraid so," said Virgil.

"And it was just like the murder a few days back?"

"Almost identical," said Wyatt.

"The killer cut off her tits?" asked Riley. "I read in the newspaper the killer cut off the other whore's tits and cut out her eyes."

"That's nonsense," said Virgil. "He cut her up pretty bad, but she still has her tits and her eyes."

"That's good," said Riley. "She had some really nice tits."

"Have you known Mary Beth to have any problems with anybody?"

"The girl had a smart mouth on her, and a temper as quick as hell," said Riley. "It's possible she could have pissed off any one of her customers. It's completely possible. She was a real firecracker, that one."

"Do you know who any of her customers were?" asked Virgil.

"Just the regulars, so far as I know."

Wyatt asked, "You wouldn't happen to know if she'd slept with that limey cocksucker Eldrich Davies, would you?"

"No," said Riley. "We wouldn't have accepted his business anyway, on account of him being Doctor Death and all."

"Wise policy," said Wyatt.

"Mary Beth got any family around here?" asked Virgil.

"No," said Riley. "Most of the whores don't, or else they wouldn't be whores."

Wyatt nodded. "Makes sense."

"If you hear anything, you be sure and let us know," said Virgil.

Now it was Riley's turn to nod. "I sure will. And you do the same."

Wyatt and Virgil left to go have another conversation with Dr. Eldrich Davies.

EIGHT
ANOTHER CHAT WITH DOCTOR DEATH

WHEN THE EARPS reached the Grand Hotel, they asked the hotel manager if Davies was up in his room. He nodded, saying, "Room 22." The Earps then made their way up the stairs, guns in hands, and the hotel manager attempted to follow them up. "No, no, no," said Virgil. "This is official police business. You stay downstairs and keep everyone calm and away from us." The hotel manager looked sad and dejected but did what he was told.

It was Wyatt who pounded on the door.

"Yes?" came the familiar voice from inside.

"Open this goddamn door, Davies."

There was a pause, and then the door was unlocked and opened. Davies looked at them, smiling a big, toothy smile.

"You better stop smiling," said Wyatt. "Or else I'm liable to knock all those pretty teeth down your goddamn throat."

Davies' smile fell away, and he looked unsure of the Earps' purpose. "I suppose you've found a new way to have me arrested," said Davies.

"There's been another murder," said Virgil, chewing on an unlit cigar.

"Another murder?" asked Davies, his face contorted.

"That's right," said Wyatt. "And we've got some questions to ask you."

"Can we come in?" asked Virgil.

Davies hesitated. "And if I were to say no?"

Wyatt said, "We'd come in anyway."

Davies swung the door wide open and walked back into the room, allowing the lawmen to follow. When they entered the hotel room, each of them scanned the place for possible clues or evidence. Wyatt walked to a table holding a chamber pot and Dr. Davies' medical bag. He reached out and grabbed the black leather bag, already unfastening its latch.

"Mind if I open this?" asked Wyatt.

"Since you're already doing it, I guess not," said Davies.

Wyatt opened the bag and dumped its contents out onto the neatly made bed. Amidst the medical tools were two scalpels. Wyatt picked one of them up and held it to the light, turning it over in his hand.

"This what you used to kill those whores?" he asked.

"Even if I had killed them with it," said Davies, "you'd never be able to prove it. As I said, I keep my utensils clean and sanitized."

"Why's that?" asked Virgil.

"In case I have to use them. I couldn't very well operate on someone with dirty utensils. That could lead to an infection."

Wyatt sat down the scalpel, picking up the second one and turning it over in his hand. "You're a very thorough man, aren't you?" he asked.

"I try to be," said Davies.

"It's very convenient that your scalpels have been cleaned

so thoroughly," said Virgil. "It makes it real hard for us to do our jobs."

"Tell me about this latest murder," said Davies.

Wyatt sneered. "As if you didn't already know."

"Humor me. Let's pretend for a moment I don't know."

"Another prostitute," said Morgan. "Killed in exactly the same way. The girl was sliced up, her abdomen cut open. And like the first girl, she was missing an ear."

Davies grinned devilishly. "What do you suppose the killer is doing with all these ears?"

Wyatt sat down the second scalpel, turned, and walked towards Davies. He got right up in the doctor's face, trying to intimidate him. While this tactic almost always worked with an adversary, Davies was completely unfazed. "Your breath is rather bad, Mr. Earp," he said, further angering Wyatt.

"Tell us about the ears, Davies," Wyatt demanded.

But Davies didn't budge. "I know nothing about any loose ears," he said.

Wyatt shoved him back against the dresser. It had to have hurt Davies, but he didn't show it. He just kept smiling that goofy grin of his, trying like hell to make them angry.

"*Tell me about the ears!*" screamed Wyatt.

"Do you figure there's a bag of ears around somewhere?" asked Davies. "Maybe the killer's made a necklace out of them, and he's wearing it around his neck. Perhaps that's the key to your investigation—simply finding a man wearing a necklace made of ears."

Wyatt reached down and touched the handle of his Schofield Smith and Wesson. "I'm gonna plug this son of a bitch right here and now." Morgan reached out and put his hand over Wyatt's, stopping him. "Let's remember what we're doing here," warned Virgil.

"I'm sorry," said Wyatt. "But this lowly bastard boils my blood."

Davies laughed heartily, as if he'd just heard the funniest joke he'd ever been told.

Wyatt backhanded him. When he did so, Davies' head didn't so much as turn. Blood came trickling down from his nostril, but Davies left it there. When the blood dripped down to his lip, he licked it, but still made no attempt to wipe it away.

"Well," said Virgil. "We're gonna have to search your room."

"For ears?" asked Davies, trying to stifle a snicker.

"Will somebody get him the hell out of here?" asked an irritated Virgil.

Wyatt turned to Morgan. "Escort him outside."

Morgan led Davies outside and closed the door behind them.

Wyatt and Virgil then began tearing the room apart. Virgil went through the dresser drawers and found a journal. "Would you look at this?" said Virgil.

"What is it?"

"It's a goddamn journal."

Wyatt reached out and snatched the book from his brother's hand, flipping through it. There was nothing inside about Davies killing anyone. However, the entry for the night of Arlene Gates' murder was nothing more than a drawn smiley face.

"What do you make of that?" asked Virgil, looking over his shoulder.

"I don't know. Could be him mocking us."

After reading about Davies' stay in jail, Wyatt came to the entry for the previous night—the night of Mary Beth Shaffer's murder. On this page was scrawled the words "GO TO HELL,

MR. EARP!" This statement was accompanied by a second smiley face.

"The bastard is taunting us," said Wyatt.

"That does appear to be the situation," said Virgil.

Wyatt looked at his brother. "You still against forcing Davies to sign that confession?"

Virgil said nothing. He just kept snooping around. He reached under Davies' pillow, his hand sliding over something. He pulled it out.

"Take a look at this," said Virgil.

Wyatt turned and looked at what Virgil had discovered—a Colt .45 revolver.

Wyatt went to the door and asked Morgan to bring the doctor back inside.

"Shut the door," he instructed Davies. Davies did.

"Well," said Davies, still grinning. "Find anything of interest?"

Virgil held up the revolver. "We found this."

Davies laughed again.

"What's so funny?" asked Wyatt.

"Since the murders were committed with a scalpel and not a pistol, that's not going to be a whole lot of help to you," said Davies.

"How do you know the murders were committed with a scalpel and not, say, a straight razor?" asked Morgan.

Davies said, "I'm just going by what you boys have told me. I'm only assuming it was a scalpel."

"What does a doctor need with a pistol?" asked Virgil.

"There a crime against that?" asked Davies. "I'm certain that dentist you go around with, Doc Holliday, has a pistol or two on him right now."

"At least that," said Wyatt.

"What do you need with a gun?" asked Virgil again.

"I need it for protection," said Davies. "After that article ran in the *Epitaph*, could be any number of people out to murder me."

"Now wouldn't that be a damned shame?" said Wyatt.

Davies looked over and saw his journal lying atop the dresser. "I see you found my journal," he said, smiling. "I do hope you had an enjoyable read, Mr. Earp."

It took everything Wyatt had not to kill the stupid bastard, but somehow, he maintained his composure.

"So, are you boys gonna arrest me or not?" asked Davies.

"I'm afraid we still have nothing to charge with you," said Virgil.

Morgan looked flustered. "What the hell, Virgil?"

Wyatt was pissed but said nothing. He just turned red and stormed out of the room.

"It looks like somebody's having a temper tantrum," said Davies.

"There were no murders while you were staying with us in the jail house," said Virgil. "I find that rather convenient. Then you get out, and all of a sudden there's another murder."

Davies kept that smile plastered across his mug. "Just lucky, I guess."

"Two things," said Virgil. "First, I'm gonna post a man downstairs in the lobby of the hotel to monitor your comings and goings. If you leave the building, he's gonna follow you wherever you go. That should keep the murders at bay."

Davies asked, "And second?"

"There's a Wells Fargo stage coming through here in a couple of days," said Virgil. "I want your ass on it. I don't care where the hell you go—you just leave Tombstone and don't ever come back."

. . .

MORGAN DIDN'T WANT to stay in the lobby of the Grand Hotel, watching for Davies. He doubted there would be any movement—especially since Virgil had tipped Davies off that he would be posted there. Morgan wanted to be where the action was. He wanted to hang out with his brothers and Doc, or see his wife, Louisa. And he was hungry. But here he was, stuck in this damnable hotel.

A sporting man Morgan barely knew named Manny Whitaker was sitting in the lobby, reading the story about Doctor Death's exploits in the *Epitaph*. He kept looking up at Morgan, obviously wanting to say something.

Finally, he did.

"Mr. Earp," he said. "I thought you should know I was playing cards with a man named Tom McLaury this morning."

Morgan had no idea what this had to do with him. "And?"

"McLaury runs with Ike Clanton and his band of cutthroats. I believe you're familiar with them. I heard your brother Wyatt had a run-in with Ike just today."

Morgan said nothing. He just listened to what the man had to say.

"McLaury was good and drunk, and he tells me he and Ike Clanton are gonna murder you and your brothers," Whitaker said. "He told me Curly Bill Brocius was gonna gun down your friend Doc Holliday. He even said they would kill your girl-friends and wives."

Morgan thought of his Louisa and started to become angry. "He say when this was supposed to happen?" he asked.

"No. Nothing specific. He just said it would happen in the next few days. He said everyone would know his and Ike's names before the week was over."

Morgan wanted to go and tell Wyatt and Virgil this news, but he couldn't leave the Grand Hotel.

Morgan asked, "What was your feeling about what he said?"

"What do you mean?"

"Did he sound like he meant it?"

"Oh yeah," Whitaker said. "He took out his Army Colt and sat it on the table. He told me, 'This is the gun that's gonna kill Wyatt Earp.' He definitely meant what he was saying." Whitaker paused for a moment. "Now whether or not he and his cowboys actually have the skills or the *cojones* to pull off such a thing is a completely different matter altogether."

Morgan just nodded.

"I don't know McLaury," said Morgan. "What's your impression of him?"

"Of McLaury? The man's a blowhard who likes hearing his own voice. Now having said that, I still believe he was serious about what he was saying. I really think he and Ike Clanton and that other no-good sumbitch Curly Bill Brocius mean to do you and your family harm."

NINE
DANGER STRIKES CLOSE TO HOME

WYATT, Virgil, and Doc were sitting at a table in the Oriental, drinking whiskey and talking things out. Big Nosed Kate was off doing her thing, and the smoke-filled saloon was doing big business. Tonight, there were no members of Ike Clanton's crew to stir up any trouble, and old Doctor Death was sealed up there in his room over at the Grand Hotel with Morgan sitting watch.

Tonight, it felt like everything was back to normal.

Hell, even Wyatt's gut was telling him everything was alright.

"It's quiet tonight," said Doc. "You can almost hear the crickets chirping."

"Thank god," said Virgil. "I'm about ready for a night of peace and quiet around here. I don't know how long it'll last, but I'm enjoying it for the moment."

Wyatt said, "I'll drink to that." He raised his glass and Doc and Virgil raised theirs. "To peace and quiet," said Doc.

"To peace and quiet," repeated Wyatt.

"I don't think it's gonna stay this way for too long," said

Virgil. "I hear there's a fella named McLaury that's been in town talking shit today."

Wyatt squinted, trying to place the name. "McLaury?"

"He's another one of Ike Clanton's gun thugs. He's been going around doing what Ike's gang does best—running his mouth. He's apparently been telling people he, Ike, and some others are gonna gun us down sometime in the next few days."

"Won't that be lovely," said Doc. "I always wanted a fall funeral."

"Maybe you'll get it," said Virgil. "McLaury's telling people Curly Bill is gonna shoot you down in the street."

Doc snickered. "Curly Bill couldn't outdraw a man with no arms. He's no threat."

"But cowboys like those don't play fair," observed Wyatt. "They don't believe in a fair fight. You fight with one of 'em, you're liable to get shot in the back by any number of other cowboys from their crew. They're some real miserable sons of bitches. They like to fight when it's five on one."

"I'm pretty sure I could get five of 'em on the draw," said Doc.

"I believe you could," said Wyatt. "I've seen you do it. But just to be careful, I think we should travel in numbers for the next few days. Let's not give those limp dick bastards the chance to get the jump on us."

"What about Morgan?" asked Doc. "He's over there at the Grand all by his lonesome."

"I know," said Virgil, "but there was no other way. I needed someone sitting over there watching Davies."

"Davies is a whole other problem," said Wyatt. "When news of Mary Beth Shaffer's murder shows up in the news-paper tomorrow, there's liable to be a whole 'nother riot."

"That's the last goddamn thing we need right now," said Virgil.

"I'll drink to that," said Doc, raising his glass.

"You'd drink to your own death, Doc," said Wyatt, grinning.

Doc smiled. "And I shall drink to that, as well, Wyatt Earp."

"Let's just hope that stagecoach comes and takes Davies out of town before vigilantes go after him again or we wind up with another dead whore on our hands," said Virgil.

"He's a talented man if he manages to kill someone else while he's being tailed by Morgan," said Doc. "If that happens, I guess we'll have to assume the man was telling the truth the whole time—that he really is innocent."

"If Eldrich Davies is innocent," Wyatt said, "then I'll be a horse's ass."

Doc laughed. "I hate to be the one to tell you this, Wyatt, but you're already a horse's ass!"

Wyatt laughed. "You got me there, Doc."

Their moment of fun was briefly interrupted when a prospector named Coates and a card shark named Handsome Harry Dempkins got into a dispute over a hand of cards. Coates stood and put his hand on his pistol, threatening to pull on Harry. Harry just laughed and kept drinking his drink, but Wyatt knew Harry had his own pistol under the table.

Wyatt approached them with his hands out in front of him. "Let's just calm down, fellas," he said. "There's no reason for anyone to die here tonight. We've all had a few drinks and I'm sure words have been exchanged. Let's let cooler heads prevail here and sit down and have another drink. Tell you what: the next round is on me, Coates."

"But he cheated me," said Coates. "This bastard here cheated me. He palmed an extra ace."

"You saw him do it?" asked Wyatt.

"No, but no man in the history of this earth has ever been so lucky as this cocksucker."

"Then why keep playing?" asked Wyatt. "Why not call it a learning experience and just walk away?"

"I done lost twenty bucks to this piece of shit."

"What if I told you I'd set you up with another twenty bucks in credit?" asked Wyatt. "Would that calm your heels? Hell, I'll even throw in a piece of pussy for free."

And that was that. Coates saw the error of his ways, even if he did still believe Handsome Harry had duped him, and he went upstairs to have sex with one of the whores. After all, he said, it was a "freebie," so why not?

After Coates had made his way upstairs, Wyatt approached Handsome Harry. "Harry," he said, "at least try to make it look right. Hell, I could see you palming cards from across the room."

Harry laughed, and Wyatt returned to his table.

"Aren't you the diplomat?" observed Doc. "And you did it without bashing a man over the head. Why, I'm right proud of you, Wyatt. It looks as if you just might be maturing after all."

Wyatt and Virgil laughed at this.

"I still say we should force Eldrich Davies to sign that confession," said Wyatt. "You and I both know we'd all feel a whole lot better if that man was swinging up there on the gallows. And for a few bucks, Judge Spicer would look the other way in the name of justice."

"Your stance on the subject is duly noted," said Virgil. "I'm just ready to get Davies out of town and let him be somebody else's problem."

Wyatt wanted to argue his point further, but he saw Joe Rucker come rushing in through the front door of the saloon. Joe looked around, stopped, and talked to someone, and they pointed over at Wyatt's table.

"It looks like we're about to have company," said Doc.

Wyatt nodded. "There goes our peace and quiet."

Joe Rucker made his way through the place, eventually finding his way to their table. He was out of breath, and he looked anxious.

"What is it, Joe?" asked Virgil.

"You fellas are needed," said Joe.

Doc asked, "What seems to be the emergency, Joe Rucker?"

"There's been another murder," he answered, looking at Wyatt. "And the killer almost got your friend—the Jewish girl."

Wyatt was on his feet before Joe Rucker could finish his sentence.

THE DEAD WHORE's name was Emma Bolinger. She was nineteen years old, and just like the other girls, her throat and abdomen had been slashed. This time, however, the killer had left his victim with both ears intact.

Wyatt, Virgil, and Doc interviewed the first witness, Chance Tucker, to ascertain what had transpired in that alleyway behind the Bird Cage Theatre. According to Tucker, he'd been walking past the mouth of the alley at Sixth Street when he'd heard a woman's screams.

"I yelled out and asked if they were alright," explained Tucker. "At first there was nothing at all, and then the Jewish girl from the theatre came running down the alley, screaming her head off. She said the killer had pushed her down behind the Bird Cage as he ran past."

"But you didn't see him?" asked Virgil.

"No, sir," said Tucker. "Well, I think I saw him moving down the alley behind the Jewish girl. He was really booking it. I think the Jewish girl must have scared the bejeezus out of him once she started screaming."

"But you couldn't make out who he was?" asked Wyatt.

"No, sir," said Tucker. "He was too far away, and really nothing more than a blurry movement in the shadows behind the girl. And at the time, she was running towards me and screaming. I didn't know what in Sam Hades was happening. It all went so fast, and the Jewish girl was crying and really shaken up by the whole thing."

"The Jewish girl," said Wyatt. "Do you know where she is now?"

"Yeah, one of the other dancers came outside and held her for a few minutes. Then they went back inside the Bird Cage. She said to have you go in there and talk to her when you showed up."

"Thanks, Tucker," said Virgil. "We really appreciate your help."

Wyatt, Virgil, and Doc walked over to look at the body under the light of Doc Goodfellow's lantern.

"Doc and I'll stay out here with Doc Goodfellow," said Virgil. "You go on inside and comfort Josephine and find out what she saw."

"I'm obliged to you for that," said Wyatt, and he turned to enter the theatre through the back door. When he walked inside the dark building, he made his way up a flight of stairs and found himself inside a well-lit dressing room. When one of the dancers saw him enter, she pointed him towards Josephine, who was sitting and talking with her friend Nora.

When she saw Wyatt, Josephine wiped away her tears and tried to be strong for him.

"Sadie," Wyatt said, now taking her in his arms.

She started to weep again.

"What happened?" asked Wyatt.

Josephine pulled back to look at him, tears in her eyes. "I went out to the alley to have a smoke. When I got down there, I

76

saw a man cutting open a woman's stomach. I startled him when the door opened, lighting the alley. He must have let his hand go from her mouth, because she let out a loud scream. The man bolted towards me. He pushed me down and took off running down the alley."

"Then what?" asked Wyatt.

She started to sob harder now. "I took off running in the opposite direction towards a man asking if everything was alright. It turned out it was that man outside, that Tucker fella."

"Everything is alright now," said Wyatt, pulling her towards him. But she pulled away, looking him in his eyes again.

"Wyatt," she said. "I saw him."

"You saw his face?" asked Wyatt, his mouth agape.

"Yes," she said. "It was that man from the newspaper."

"Eldrich Davies?"

"Yeah, that's him," she said. "Doctor Death."

Wyatt asked, "Are you sure?"

"Yes, I'm quite sure. I'll see his face in my nightmares."

Wyatt pushed himself back. "Sadie, I've got to go. Virgil and I have to go and put that bastard behind bars so he can swing for he done."

And Wyatt was gone.

WYATT, Virgil, and Doc ran towards the Grand Hotel as quickly as they could. When they finally got there, they all rushed into the front door of the establishment. They found Morgan sitting there just inside the door, watching the stairs. There was no one else in the lobby.

"There's been another murder," said Virgil.

"The son of a bitch hurt Josephine," said Wyatt. "Why did you let him go?"

There was an expression of shock on Morgan's face. "He never left here. I been here all night, and I haven't seen Davies once."

Wyatt spun around and took off up the stairs towards Davies' room. When he got there, he knocked. Getting no answer, he stepped back and ran towards the door, breaking it open.

The room was empty, and the window was open.

Davies was gone.

TEN
DAVIES ON THE RUN

THE EARP BROTHERS and Doc Holliday walked out of the Grand Hotel with no idea where the hell the killer was. At first, they considered each of them going his separate way in search of Davies, but then it was decided that they should split up into two groups. Virgil and Morgan went one way, and Wyatt and Doc went the other.

Wyatt and Doc walked slowly through the darkened streets of Tombstone. There wasn't much going on out here. The wind was kicking up dust, and there were a few people, mostly on foot, passing to and fro in the darkness.

Wyatt and Doc stopped around at establishments like the Alhambra and the Hafford, asking patrons if they had seen Dr. Davies. No one had. Wyatt and Doc slowly made their way towards the Cochise County Courthouse, walking up Fourth Street, and checking in every nook and cranny they came to.

They had just passed Spangenberg's Cosmopolitan Hotel when they spotted a figure walking along the building fronts, sporting a bowler hat like Davies'. They both pulled out their pistols, approaching slowly from behind. When they were about twenty feet behind the man, Wyatt yelled out, "Davies!" The man turned around, and even in the darkness they could see it was him.

Davies took off running in the direction of the courthouse.

As they ran, Wyatt kept thinking, *This son of a bitch hurt my Sadie.* This recurring thought made him angrier and angrier, spurring him to run even when he was out of breath. For a man who looked as weak as Davies did, he did an impressive job running from them without pause. Even more impressive was Doc, who suffered from consumption, running nonstop after the man they called Doctor Death.

Wyatt considered firing at Davies but thought the better of it. He wanted the chance to beat the living hell out of him before watching him swing up on those gallows.

But Davies turned and opened fire on them. His shot struck something to Wyatt's right and careened off down the street.

Wyatt, still running, fired off a couple of volleys, but Davies just kept running. Finally, Doc stopped. "I'm tired of all this goddamn running," he said, raising both arms and firing his Colt Thunderer and his Colt Lightning simultaneously. Doc only fired twice, but Davies went down hard, dropping his medical bag.

As they approached Davies, Wyatt yelled out, "Drop the gun or else we'll kill you right here and now!" Davies tossed the pistol away from him into the street. Out of breath, Davies managed, "I'm unarmed."

Wyatt walked towards him and started kicking the hell out of him.

As he did so, he said, "Eldrich Davies, you are under arrest for the murders of those three whores." And he just kept on kicking Davies until finally Doc stopped him. "Save something for the gallows, Wyatt," said Doc.

. . .

Dr. Eldrich Davies was sitting in his cell at the jail house, recovering from a wound in his right leg, three broken ribs, and a bruised and battered face. Doc Goodfellow had already been in to remove the bullet, and Wyatt had allowed Doc Goodfellow the opportunity to punch Davies in the face once.

"Damn, that felt good," the old man had said. "I think I busted my hand pretty good, but it was completely worth it."

Now Doc Goodfellow was gone, and Wyatt was standing over Davies outside the bars.

Wyatt was trembling with anger.

"You and I are gonna have us one hell of a good time tonight," said Wyatt. He unlocked the cell and ordered Morgan to pull Davies out. Morgan went into the cell and grabbed Davies, throwing him hard to the floor. He then reached down and dragged him out towards Virgil's chair.

"Sit his ass up in that chair," said Wyatt.

Morgan helped Davies stand, and then sat him back in the chair.

"You aren't gonna break my new chair, are you?" asked Virgil.

Wyatt grinned. "We can always get you a new chair, Virg. Hell, I'll get you two."

Morgan shackled the injured prisoner to the chair so he could not try to escape, not that Davies could have tried even if he'd wanted to. Once Davies was attached to the chair, Wyatt took off his belt. He turned to Virgil. "Lock the door, Virg."

Wyatt swung the leather strap high in the air and brought it down hard against Davies' body, lashing him with it. He did this several times, even managing to whip the belt across Davies' face a couple times for good measure.

"That woman you pushed down in the alley?" Wyatt said. "That was my friend. That was my Sadie..." His voice trailed off before his anger reanimated him. *"That was my goddamn Sadie!"*

Davies had been beaten so long and so hard he didn't even put up a fight.

He didn't even ask what exactly he'd been arrested for.

In fact, all he did was bleed.

And hurt.

Now it was Morgan's turn. Morgan bit off the end of a nice, fat cigar, and lit it, puffing it hard as he did. Once he had a good burn going, he pressed the lit cigar against Davies' neck. The cigar made a sickening sizzling sound as it burned its way into Davies' soft flesh, sinking in like a knife in hot butter. Davies cried out in agony. Then Morgan puffed on the cigar a few more times, took it out of his mouth and blew softly on its burning embers. Davies just sat there with his head down, whimpering. Then Morgan took Davies' right hand—the one that would have cut those whores—and burned the cigar into its meat. Davies screamed out again.

Now it was Virgil's turn.

"You could have made all this much easier on yourself," said Virgil. "You could have just confessed, and it would have been over. But no, you had to go and kill two more whores. You just had to do it. And you had to mock us. You know how that makes us feel, Eldrich?" He paused. "Can I call you Eldrich?"

Davies tried to look up through bloodied, slitted eyes, but said nothing.

"You made us look bad," said Virgil. "And that I cannot abide. That and killing them whores."

Virgil took out his Colt .45 and whipped Davies with it.

Then he did it again, two of Davies' teeth flying from his mouth as he did so.

Now it was Wyatt's turn again...

ELEVEN
JUSTICE

JUDGE WELLS SPICER oversaw the proceedings at the Cochise County Courthouse.

"I understand there is a signed confession," said Spicer. "Is that correct?"

"That is correct," said Wyatt.

Eldrich Davies, representing himself because no one else would take his case, attempted to speak out about the nature of his confession, but Spicer told him to shut the fuck up until he was spoken to.

Spicer read Davies' confession out loud before the court. "I, Dr. Eldrich Davies, being of sound mind and body, do hereby confess to having brutally murdered the three whores, Arlene Gates, Mary Beth Shaffer, and Emma Bolinger. I did so because I am a scurrilous son of a bitch who does not believe in god..." Judge Spicer stopped reading and looked up at the Earps, knowing full well the nature of Davies' confession, but said nothing. He then continued reading, "I, Dr. Eldrich Davies, do hereby throw myself on the mercy of the court."

Spicer then called Josephine Marcus up to the stand for

good measure. He had her swear in over the good book. She then testified as to what she had seen in the alleyway that night behind the Bird Cage Theatre.

Almost the exact moment Josephine had finished her testimony, the courthouse erupted with chants of "string him up!" In what would be the shortest murder trial of Judge Wells Spicer's career, it took him a mere twelve minutes to read and listen to the testimony and ultimately pass judgment on Davies.

"Dr. Eldrich Davies," Spicer said, "I hereby sentence you to be hung by the neck until you are dead. May God have mercy on your heathen soul."

Perhaps Davies still wanted to speak and have his proverbial day in court, but no one will ever know because someone threw a large rock and struck him in the head, rendering him unconscious.

The perpetrator who threw the rock was never found.

THE GALLOWS WERE CONSTRUCTED in quick time in a lot out by the miner's cabins off Tough Nut Street. When the day of the big event came, more than six hundred people showed up to witness Davies' impending death. The large crowd consisted not only of Tombstone residents, but also those of nearby towns such as San Simon, Charleston, and Galeyville.

Vendors sold sweet confections and beverages there, and both the *Epitaph* and the *Nugget* would later report that a good time was had by all who attended. Throughout the hour leading up to the hanging, chants of "string him up" and "Doctor Death" would alternate, with entire families getting in on the act.

The Earps and their families were all in attendance. Wyatt had instructed Josephine not to attend as he said executions were no place for a woman. But really, he just did this because he was bringing his common law wife Mattie with him. (Mattie had insisted on going, and there was nothing Wyatt could do to stop her.)

Virgil Earp escorted Dr. Eldrich Davies out onto the scaffold at approximately six a.m. "Dr. Eldrich Davies," he said, "Do you have any last words before you depart this world?"

"There is only one thing I would like to say," said Davies. A hush fell over the crowd momentarily as everyone waited to see what this terrible man had to say. And this is what he said: *"Fuck you all!"*

The crowd went crazy, and the roaring chants of "string him up" became deafening. A gunny sack was placed over Davies' head, the rope was tightened around his neck, and he was left to stand there awaiting his death for what must have seemed like an eternity. Now the crowd was quiet again. When Virgil finally pulled the lever, dropping the kicking man from the gallows, everyone in the crowd began to cheer again.

Everyone watched as Davies' kicking started to slow.

And finally, he kicked no more.

At this, Mayor John Clum stepped up onto the scaffold and announced, "Today justice has been served!"

And the crowd went wild.

TWELVE
THE AFTERMATH

THE VERY NEXT MORNING, Wyatt came to Josephine's hotel room. His knocking awoke her from her slumber. She arose and answered the door, pleased to find her man standing before her.

"Sadie," he said, "I have important business to attend to. It's likely to be extremely dangerous. Some very bad men who want my brothers and me dead are waiting for us down at the O.K. Corral. There may be gunplay. I hope not, but we're prepared for the worst."

"Will Doc be with you?" she asked.

"Yes," said Wyatt.

"Good," she said. "Tell him I said to keep you safe."

"I have to go now. Stay here in your room and you should be safe. If anyone comes knocking, don't answer the door, no matter who it is. Do you understand?"

"Yes," she said. "Wyatt, I'm frightened."

He took her in his arms, and he kissed her like there would be no tomorrow. He then pulled back and said, "I'll take care of you, Sadie."

"You promise you'll be back?"

He hesitated, unsure as to whether or not he would live through the day, but he said, "I promise, Sadie. I promise I'll be back." He kissed her hard, turned, and walked out through the door.

He turned one last time. "Be sure and lock the door," he said.

She blew a kiss to him. "Be safe, my love," she said.

And Wyatt was gone.

JOSEPHINE LOCKED THE DOOR. She hoped and prayed her man would be safe from those ruffians who wished to hurt him.

She moved towards her dresser and pulled the drawer open. She then moved her undergarments aside. She reached in and grabbed the straight razor which had once belonged to her former beau Johnny Behan, along with the tiny satin pouch. She raised it in the hand which held the razor and pulled at the pouch's drawstrings to open it. She looked inside at the two dried and bloodied ears it held and vowed to get rid of them while Wyatt was handling his business at the O.K. Corral. Yes, she thought, she would feed the ears to the hogs just down the street.

Now everything would be alright, she thought.

She and Wyatt would be happy together, and all her troubles would be behind her. She hadn't felt the feeling—that sickening, overpowering urge to kill—since she'd resided in San Francisco a few years prior. There she had taken the lives of two whores, but she hadn't gotten fancy with it. She was still learning. Because there was nothing special about the two murders—their throats had been slashed, and that was it—no one had ever connected them as being the work of the same person. And she had walked away from those murders scot-free, vowing never to do such a heinous thing again.

But then she had come to Tombstone, and those old familiar urges came to her once again. She knew it was wrong, but when she took a life, she felt stronger than any woman had ever felt before. She felt immortal. She was fearless. In a funny way, she now believed the murders had been the cause of the outspoken, free-spirited demeanor she now carried with her. These were the very qualities which had caused Wyatt Earp to fall in love with her, so it couldn't be all that bad, could it?

He was her Wyatt, and she was his Sadie.

Together they would take on the world.

Together they would be happy.

Together they were one.

EMMETT DALTON RIDES AGAIN!

Dedicated to Leo Rausch.

A decent cowboy does not take what belongs to someone else, and if he does, he deserves to be strung up and left for the flies and coyotes.

—Judge Roy Bean

I rob banks for a living. What do you do?

—John Dillinger

ONE

OUTLAWS NEVER DIE

It was 1933, and Emmett Dalton, notorious bank robber from the Old West, was now long retired from his life of crime. After the 1892 dual bank robbery in Coffeyville, Kansas, which had made him a legend, he'd done a fourteen-year stretch in the pen out in Lansing. That stint had provided him with plenty of time to reflect on all the mistakes he'd made as a younger man, and he had vowed never to make them again.

But damned if he wasn't jealous of these youngsters. When he read about these kids like John Dillinger, Baby Face Nelson, and Bonnie and Clyde in the newspapers, he found himself longing to raise a little hell. But he was an old man now. He was sixty-two, and robbing banks was a young man's game. Who the hell had ever heard of a geriatric bank robber?

Today Emmett was an author with a couple of autobiographies under his belt and was also a bit movie actor. Life was pretty damned good. He had no time for such nonsense as robbing banks, but that didn't stop him from daydreaming about it every now and again.

He was sitting at a table in the Brown Derby Restaurant across from his would-be biographer, Harrison Bennett. Harrison, whom Emmett guessed to be in his mid-thirties, worshipped him as some kind of a hero.

"Look," Emmett said, chewing a piece of steak. "Those stories are great. They make me out to be the greatest thing since Moses parted the Red Sea. People call me a living legend. But the truth is, those stories have been greatly exaggerated over the years. They're bullshit. Sure, I've managed to make a living trading on those old tales, but they just ain't true. I'm no more a hero than you are, son. I was a very bad man, Harrison, and I don't deserve to be seen as anything more."

Harrison scribbled in his little notepad.

"Why don't you take a break and eat your food," Emmett suggested. "It's getting cold."

"What was it really like pulling that bank robbery—the one that ended the Dalton Gang?" asked Harrison.

Emmett looked at him, a grim expression on his face. "Two of my brothers was gunned down in the street. It wasn't the best day of my life. It's the one day I'm always gonna be remembered for, but I've seen better days than that one."

"But the robbery itself—was it a rush?"

That was when Harrison saw a glint in the old man's eye. "It was a hell of a time robbing those banks. For the record, I was against it from the start. I said, 'Robbing two banks at the same time is just plain stupid. And on top of that, it's greedy.' But you know how bank robbers are, they didn't listen. In the end, everyone in the gang wanted to do it but me, so I figured what the hell and went right along with 'em."

"Do you regret it?"

"Hell yes, I regret it," said Emmett. "The robbery itself was as fun as could be, but when we got out of that bank... That was a whole 'nother story. There must have been thirty men out there with guns trained on us."

"And you got shot," said Harrison. "Is that right?"

"You're damned right I got shot. I got shot twenty-three times. Can you believe that? The Lord must have been lookin' out for me. Hell, I'll bet every one of those sons of bitches that was standin' out there caught me with a bullet that day. Twenty-three bullets! Can you believe that? Here we are all these years later, and I still can't believe it."

Harrison took a drink of his coffee. "I'll bet that hurt like hell."

"I can't even begin to tell you how badly those wounds hurt," said Emmett. "And you know what? When I got to the doc's office, he was talking about me like I wasn't even there. They were all saying how I was already as good as dead. One of 'em said something to the effect of, 'Piss on 'em. Who cares if he lives anyway?' It was a really rough time. But I'll be damned if I didn't show 'em all. I lived, goddammit. Here I am sitting here with you all these years later, drinking this terrible fuckin' coffee, and I'm still alive."

"Is there anyone else from the Dalton Gang who's still alive?" asked Harrison.

"Shit no," said Emmett. "I am, as they say, the last of the Mohicans. I'm the last man standing." Now he turned the questioning around. "So, tell me about this book you're writing. What's it gonna be called?"

"I was thinking about titling it *Outlaws Never Die*. What do you think?"

"I think that's one hell of a misleading title. Outlaws *do* die, and the Daltons were proof. We, and I mean as a group now, did that better than anything else—die. Well, everyone but me, I guess. I never was good at much of anything." Emmett laughed.

"Should I change the title?" asked Harrison, a concerned look on his face.

"You can title it that if you want. Hell, it's got a better ring to it than the titles of the books I wrote," said Emmett.

Harrison smiled. "I really enjoyed your books. Especially *Beyond the Law*."

"Thanks, but like I said, it was all crap."

"All of it?"

"Enough of it."

"Well, I wanna tell the truth in this book," said Harrison. "I want to tell it the way it really was."

"They'll never buy it," Emmett said flatly. "People don't want the truth. They'd rather have the legend."

Visibly uncomfortable, Harrison changed the subject. "So, what do you think about all these robbers running around today?"

"You mean like Johnny Dillinger and all those folks?"

"Yeah," said Harrison. "People like Ma Barker's gang and so on."

"There sure are a lot of them all of a sudden," observed Emmett. "It's just like it was back in our day..." He stared off out the window for a second, and then turned back to Harrison. "I forgot—what was your question?"

Harrison smiled, chewing a bite from his rock-hard dinner roll. "I asked what you thought about these contemporary bank robbers?"

"For the most part I don't like 'em," said Emmett. "You know why?"

"No, why?"

"Because they got no style. They got no panache. You take a guy like Baby Face Nelson or Pretty Boy Floyd. They carry Tommy Guns, and they can shoot fifteen, twenty sons of bitches at a time with those things. They got no finesse. Boy, if

we'd had Tommy Guns when we came out of that bank in Coffeyville, we'd have gotten away scot-free. No question about it. But you know what? Nobody's gonna remember any of 'em the way people remember us; the way they remember Jesse James' gang; the way they remember the Wild Bunch."

"You think so?" asked Harrison.

"I know so," said Emmett. "One of these days Johnny Law is gonna catch up with 'em and plant 'em all in their graves. And you know why? Because that man Melvin Purvis and those G-men of his, they got Tommy guns, too. And when that day comes, you mark my words, people are gonna forget all about these contemporary outlaws of yours. Why? They got no style." He paused and took a sip from his coffee. "But you know who I do like?"

"Who?" asked Harrison.

"That goddamn John Dillinger. Now there's a bank robber's got some style about him. They say he robs banks, and he tells 'em they should be thankful to have been robbed by him because, as he tells it, he's the greatest bank robber ever lived."

"You believe that?" asked Harrison. "That he's the greatest bank robber of all time?"

"No, and I doubt he believes it either. But the man's got style, and he has confidence. People just might remember him someday the way they remember us. We'll just have to wait and see."

"I think you might be right," said Harrison, agreeing with him as usual.

"So, when do you wanna meet up and talk again?" asked Emmett.

"How about Wednesday afternoon?"

Emmett nodded. "Wednesday should be fine. It's not like I'm gonna have anything to do."

But he was wrong.

ANDY RAUSCH

. . .

THAT NIGHT, with visions of bank robbers still dancing around
in his head, Emmett read an account of John Dillinger's latest
exploits in the *Los Angeles Times*. In the same issue, Emmett
also read a story about a former Old West outlaw like himself
named Jimmy McDaniels. McDaniels had run with the Jesse
Evans Gang, robbing banks and stagecoaches back in the
1870s. According to the "where-are-they-now?" piece Emmett
was reading, McDaniels was now 78 years old and staying in a
place called Seven Rivers, New Mexico, where he was living as
a retired real estate agent.

"I'll be damned," said Emmett aloud.

"What?" asked his wife, Julia, who was sitting next to him,
reading the latest issue of *The Reader's Digest*.

Emmett turned to her and said, "Nothing, dear."

And the wheels in Emmett's head started to turn.

AFTER LISTENING to "The George Gershwin Show," Emmett
and Julia retired to bed. Julia fell asleep within a matter of
minutes, but Emmett found himself restless and unable to
sleep. Thoughts of Jimmy McDaniels, John Dillinger, and his
own legacy kept racing through his head.

And he knew.

At that moment he knew with absolute certainty that he
wanted to rob another bank or two before he died. This was
significant because it was the first time he'd ever considered
such a thing as a real possibility. He'd always missed the thrill
of robbing banks, but he'd just assumed that life was now
behind him.

But what if it wasn't?

What if he was to go down there and meet with old Jimmy

McDaniels? What if he was to ask McDaniels to join him in robbing banks? Would McDaniels do it? The answer was likely no, especially since McDaniels was getting up there in years. But what could it hurt to go and meet with the man? Emmett had always believed himself to have good luck, as evidenced by his surviving the Coffeyville fiasco, and he felt confident he could persuade that old outlaw to join forces with him. If McDaniels were to say yes to his proposal, then maybe the two of them could show these young fellas how it was really done.

Emmett lay there considering all this for a number of hours. Finally, just after three, he got up and went to the kitchen. There he brewed some coffee and sat down and read that article about Jimmy McDaniels again. *Perhaps*, he thought. *Maybe this could really work.*

After considering this for a few moments, Emmett stood and went to the closet in the living room and pulled out a suitcase. He crept to the bedroom where Julia was sleeping and removed several sets of clothing, bringing them back out into the kitchen and packing them in the bag.

It was now just after four.

Emmett went to the bathroom and ran himself some water. He then took a quick bath in preparation for his impending trip. Once he was finished, he climbed out of the tub, dried himself off, and put on a fresh set of duds. He wrote out a long letter to his wife, telling her he would be gone for a while. The letter was intentionally vague, as Emmett didn't want her to put two and two together. He positioned the letter prominently on the dining room table so she would be sure to see it.

Emmett snuck back into the bedroom and kissed his sleeping wife's forehead. "I'll see you soon," he whispered. He turned and went back into the bedroom closet, retrieving an old shoebox from the top shelf. He held the box closed in his hands for a moment, knowing full well that once that particular Pandora's box was opened it could never be closed again.

He opened the box and removed his .44-40 caliber Colt single-action revolver. He held it up, looking at it. He felt at home with the gun in his hand. It felt as though he had never even put it away.

TWO

HOOLINGANISM AND CAMERADERIE

IT WAS ROUGHLY a thousand miles to Seven Rivers, New Mexico, and Emmett hoped to make it all in a single drive with no significant stops. He stopped his black 1931 Ford Model A coupe a number of times to purchase gasoline or stretch his legs, and he made the drive in roughly twenty-three hours.

When he got to Seven Rivers, he had no idea where the hell Jimmy McDaniels lived. It was still the middle of the night and there was nothing going on in town, so he napped in the car until nine. He planned to go to the newspaper office to inquire about McDaniels' whereabouts, but soon learned that Seven Rivers did not have its own newspaper. Instead, it relied on publications from surrounding cities Artesia and Carlsbad. He stopped at a filling station and offered the pump attendant ten bucks for information on McDaniels.

"Hell, everyone knows old Jimmy McDaniels," said the attendant. "He's kind of a big deal around here."

The attendant took the ten and gave Emmett directions to the real estate office where McDaniels had once worked. Ned

Fremont, the agent working at the office, was more than happy to give Emmett directions to McDaniels' home.

Emmett drove a few blocks over to where the former outlaw now resided. When he got there, he pulled the coupe into the circle driveway, parking it next to another Model A. He straightened his suit, checked out his reflection in the automobile's window to make sure he looked right, and stepped up to the porch.

He knocked on the door several times. Finally, an elderly man with a pot belly and a bulbous nose opened it. Emmett recognized McDaniels from the photograph that had run alongside the man's profile in the *Times*.

"Can I help you?" McDaniels asked, still standing half in and half out the door.

Emmett extended his hand. "Pleased to meet you, sir. My name is Emmett Dalton."

McDaniels' eyes grew big as saucers. "Emmett Dalton?" he asked. "As in *the* Emmett Dalton?"

"I sure hope I'm *the* Emmett Dalton," said Emmett, grinning. "I don't believe this world could handle two of us."

For a moment, McDaniels was a child again. He reached out and grabbed Emmett's hand, pumping it hard. "I'm pleased to make your acquaintance," he said. "You can call me Jimmy."

He then opened the door and stepped back, allowing Emmett entrance. When Emmett walked into the house and got a good look at it, he instantly felt at home. The walls were covered with framed photographs and newspaper clippings about Jimmy's exploits as a bank robber. His old cowboy hat was hanging there, and his Colt .45 Peacemaker was on display in a glass cabinet.

"I love what you've done with the place," remarked Emmett.

"I kept *everything*," Jimmy said. "My dear departed wife, Sally, used to say I was a packrat. I guess she was right."

As Emmett surveyed Jimmy's own personal outlaw museum, he came to a bookshelf filled with books on the Old West. Scanning them, he saw his own books, *Beyond the Law* and *When the Daltons Rode*.

"Yeah," Jimmy said happily. "I got both your books."

"Well," managed Emmett, "I guess there's no accounting for taste."

Jimmy walked into the next room. "Why don't you follow me into the kitchen so we can talk." He turned back to Emmett. "Can I get you something to drink?"

"Please."

"What would you like? Coffee? Tea?"

Emmett asked, "You got any spirits?"

"It's only ten o'clock," said Jimmy. "You start that early?"

"For what I got to say, we're gonna need spirits."

Jimmy tilted his head, wondering what was coming. "Well, you've certainly piqued my interest, Mr. Dalton." He motioned for Emmett to sit at the table, and he went to the cabinet to get the scotch and a couple of glasses. He sat down and poured them both a drink.

Emmett downed his immediately.

Jimmy grinned. "Some things never change, I guess."

"You don't know the half."

"So, what can I do for you?"

"I want to talk to you about something."

"I surmised as much."

Emmett looked him in the eyes. "Do you ever miss it?"

"Miss what?" asked Jimmy, now sipping his own drink.

"Being an outlaw," Emmett said. "The hooliganism and the camaraderie."

"Of course I do. Those were the greatest times of my life. How about you?"

Emmett smiled. "Every goddamn day."

Jimmy smiled, too.

"I wanna talk to you about startin' a new gang," said Emmett.

Jimmy almost fell out of his chair. *"What?"*

"I'm serious as a heart attack."

"My God, man," said Jimmy. "I'm seventy-eight years old!"

"I know. That's why it's perfect. They'll never see us coming."

Jimmy stared at him, pouring himself another scotch. He downed it.

"You're serious, aren't you?"

"Yes, sir, I am," said Emmett. "What do you think?"

"I think you're out of your damn fool mind, Emmett Dalton."

"So that's a 'no' then?" asked Emmett.

Jimmy raised his hand. "Now I didn't say that. It just so happens that I'm just as crazy an old fool as you are. This is an interesting proposition, Mr. Dalton. Yes, indeed. But how did you choose me?"

"Everyone else was dead."

Jimmy chuckled. "You can say that again." He poured them both another drink and raised his glass in toast. "To dead outlaws!" Emmett raised his glass, and they both threw back their drinks.

"So, you're gonna do it?" asked Emmett.

"Are you kidding? I been waitin' forty years for you to walk through my door and ask me this."

Emmett couldn't believe what he was hearing. He'd been prepared to try and convince Jimmy, and it turned out the man didn't need persuading. "You don't need to mull it over?"

"What's to mull over?" asked Jimmy. "I got nothing else to live for, and I'm damn near dead. Docs say I got cancer in my bones. I won't live more than two or three years at best. So, let's do this thing, Emmett Dalton. Let's go out there and show these little bastards robbin' all these banks how real bank robbers do it."

AFTER JIMMY MCDANIELS had packed all his clothes, he said, "Just one thing left to pack."

"What's that?" asked Emmett.

"Come on," said Jimmy, leading him through the house. "I'll show you."

He led him down the hall, past the bathroom and his own bedroom to what would normally be a guest bedroom. Jimmy opened the door and walked in. Emmett followed.

The room was filled with guns of all shapes and sizes, mounted on the walls There must have been fifteen different shotguns and thirty-five, forty pistols there. This crazy son of a bitch Jimmy had his own little armory.

"Would you look at that," managed Emmett.

"Yeah, it's a hobby of mine. I been collecting guns for more than twenty years now."

Emmett couldn't believe his eyes. "They're beautiful."

"Take what you like, partner," said Jimmy, beaming like a proud father. "I'll be taking my old Colt .45 Peacemaker from the front room, as well as this Colt Dragoon here and a coach gun or two."

Emmett scanned the collection of shotguns, looking as beautiful as the day on which they'd been produced. "Mind if I take this sawed-off 10-gauge?"

"Take whatever you like. So long as we're partners, you're

free to use anything I got. What's mine is yours, Emmett Dalton."

Emmett said, "That sounds damn fine to me."

"One more thing."

"What?"

"We're gonna need a few extra guns."

"Why?"

Jimmy grinned. "That's what I wanna talk to you about."

THE TWO MEN were back in the kitchen, sitting at the table, finishing off the bottle of scotch. There were guns all around them, pistols on the table, pistols on their person, shotguns leaning against the wall.

"I got a friend by the name of Tom Pickett," said Jimmy. "You ever hear of him?"

"Can't say as I have."

"Tom was an outlaw like us."

"Who'd he ride with?" asked Emmett, pouring himself a drink.

"He rode with Dave Rudabaugh."

Emmett asked, "Dirty Dave Rudabaugh?"

"Same. Then later he rode with Billy the Kid."

Emmett nodded, turning it over in his mind. There were definitely advantages to having a third man in the gang. The main disadvantage was that they'd have to share part of the money. But hell, neither of them was doing this for the money. No, they were doing it to regain a piece of their youth, and a man couldn't put a price on that.

"How old is this guy?" asked Emmett.

"He just had a birthday," said Jimmy. "I think he turned seventy-five, but don't hold me to that. He might be seventy-six."

"What else can you tell me about him?"

"He used to be a lawman—part of the Dodge City Gang out in Vegas. After that, he was a lawman here in New Mexico."

"He still live here?"

Jimmy smiled. "No, he doesn't. That's the other thing I wanted to talk to you about."

"Okay," said Emmett. "What is it?"

Jimmy was lighting his pipe, and he waited until he had it going well before he spoke. Finally, he said, "He lives in Joplin, Missouri. Ever hear of it?"

Emmett nodded. "Yeah."

"Well, think of it this way—all the banks a gang could knock over are out there in the Midwest," said Jimmy, puffing on his pipe. "In fact, there's a bank there in Joplin that's been hit three or four times this year alone. I believe Machine Gun Kelly, Dillinger, and the Barrows Gang all knocked it over."

"You sure it's safe to hit it again?"

"Those stupid bastards don't learn," said Jimmy. "They keep thinkin' surely they won't get hit again, and then they do. It's an easy job. Easy-peezy."

Emmett thought about it. "So, you wanna go get this guy Pickett in Joplin?"

"I do," Jimmy said. "We're gonna need a third man anyway. It takes two men to hit the bank and a third to drive."

"Times have changed. Last time I robbed a bank, we were riding horses."

Jimmy laughed. "Me too. But horses die when they get shot."

"And automobiles explode," said Emmett. "That's not really reassuring."

"Well," said Jimmy, "I reckon we could take horses to do

the job, but I think the law would catch up to us pretty damn quick."

Emmett laughed now. "I was just joshin'. I love horses, but I don't miss ridin' 'em everywhere. Seems like I always had sore balls back then."

Jimmy laughed. "I don't miss that either."

"So, I guess we're heading to Missouri," said Emmett.

"Yeah," said Jimmy. "I guess we are."

"There's one place I wanna stop on the way. One bank I wanna knock over."

"With just the two of us?"

"Yeah."

"Where's that?"

Emmett grinned. "Coffeyville, Kansas."

THREE
COFFEYVILLE, KANSAS

THE LONG JOURNEY from New Mexico to Coffeyville took
two full days, with each of them taking turns at the wheel.
Emmett was driving when they passed through Tulsa, Okla-
homa. He was now only about eighty miles away from the town
where he'd made his mark. As he drove on, his mind turned to
Julia. He was sure she would be sick with worry, and he now
felt bad for having left her in the dark about all this. But the
truth was, Julia was a God-fearing Christian woman, and she
would not have approved of all this craziness.

Having been asleep for the past six hours, Jimmy began to
stir. "Where we at?"

"We're close," said Emmett. "We just passed Tulsa."

"I never been to Tulsa," remarked Jimmy. "I woulda liked
to have seen it."

"You ain't missing much. It's a big city, sure, but it's
changed so much since I was there last. It don't even look like it
could be the same city."

Jimmy nodded. "Everything's changed."

"Everything but us."

Jimmy smiled at this truth. "So, what's it like in Coffeyville?"

"Well hell, I ain't been there in forty-one years. How the hell should I know?"

"Isn't Walter Johnson from there? I seem to recall he was."

"Walter Johnson, the ball player?" asked Emmett. "He's from Coffeyville?"

"Seems like I read that somewhere."

"Well, I guess everybody's gotta be from somewhere."

"You a baseball fan?"

"Just in passing," said Emmett.

"Does Walter Johnson still play?"

"He's a manager now."

"With the Senators?"

"Used to be, but now he's over there in Cleveland."

They drove on, soon approaching the Verdigris River, which meant they were close now. They came to the small suburb of South Coffeyville, and Emmett could feel his anticipation building with every passing minute.

"What do you wanna do in Coffeyville, aside from the obvious?" asked Jimmy.

"We could go to a show," said Emmett. "Man on the radio said that *King Kong* picture is pretty good."

"Supposed to be scary?"

Emmett said, "I guess."

"Let's rob the bank first."

"Then go to a show?"

"Why not?"

And on they drove.

LAST TIME he'd been in Coffeyville, Emmett and his brothers had attempted to rob the First National Bank and the C.M.

Condon Bank at the same time. But now, all these years later, the C. M. Condon was gone, leaving only the First National to rob.

Now here they were, sitting outside the bank in the coupe.

"We really need a third man to drive," said Jimmy.

"Third man shit," said Emmett. "We can do this with just the two of us."

"You think?"

"Hell yes. We were built for this, son."

"We just leave the Ford running?"

"Yeah."

In the old days, both men would have spent the minutes leading up to a robbery getting themselves psyched for the event. Today, however, they were older and wiser, and each man remained calm and collected.

Emmett had the big .44-40 caliber Colt revolver in his hand, ready to go. Jimmy had both of his pistols holstered in a fancy black two-gun rig and was carrying the 12-gauge.

Now was the time.

"You ready for this?" asked Emmett, his hand on the door handle.

"Ready as I'm ever gonna be, I reckon."

The two old outlaws stepped out of the Ford. There was no one on the sidewalk, and no cars moving in the street around them. This was gonna be a piece of cake. Easy-peasy, just as Jimmy had said.

Moving towards the entrance, Emmett said, "I'll take lead." He swung the door open and rushed inside. Jimmy was right behind. There were only three customers in the place. Everyone in the room saw them at the same time.

Emmett raised the Colt. "Alright everybody, this here is a robbery!"

No one knew what to do. All the people in the bank looked

around for cues. Finally, Jimmy yelled out, "Everyone down on the floor! *Now!*"

Emmett rushed ahead to the front counter with Jimmy standing back at the door. Just when Emmett reached the counter, another bank employee, a frumpy, middle-aged woman wearing too much makeup, stepped out of the vault to see what was happening.

"You!" Emmett said, catching her off guard. "Take out all the money from the drawers and put it in a bag." He looked back at Jimmy, who was surveying the room. So far so good. Emmett turned back to the woman. "Who's the bank manager?"

The woman pointed down at the floor where a skinny, balding man in a suit was lying. "That's Lenny right there," she said. "He's the manager."

"Lenny, get on your feet," said Emmett.

Lenny looked up nervously, slowly raising himself off the ground.

"Take me to the vault now."

Lenny turned towards the open vault. Emmett briefly considered trying to jump up and over the counter, but he knew he couldn't make it. As Lenny the bank manager stood waiting at the mouth of the vault, Emmett walked down around the counter.

Old Lenny here was nervous as all hell, but he didn't put up a fight. He just unlocked the door and walked inside the vault.

So far so good, Emmett thought.

"I want you to take as much cash as you can get ahold of and stick it in a couple of bags," said Emmett. Lenny nodded and went to work. Emmett waited nervously as the bank manager filled two bags with cash. Finally, the man handed over the bags, filled to the brim with cash.

"Thank you, sir," said Emmett. "Now you stay here."

"In the vault?"

"In the vault."

Emmett walked back to the woman at the counter and picked up the third bag of money, holding them all in the same hand. "You didn't hit the alarm, did you?" he asked.

She shook her head.

Emmett raised the Colt into the air so everyone could see it and said, "You have just been robbed by the Emmett Dalton gang! So, when someone asks who it was that took your money, you can tell 'em proudly it was Emmett Dalton and Jimmy McDaniels."

When the customers and employees heard the name Dalton, they all gasped collectively.

"Hey," someone said. Emmett looked over and saw the fat, old security guard lying on the floor near Jimmy's feet. He was looking up at him.

"What do you want, fat man?" asked Emmett.

The man was grinning. "You're Emmett Dalton?"

"Yes, sir," said Emmett proudly.

"I was working here way back when you sons of bitches robbed this bank the first time," the security guard said.

Emmett and Jimmy exchanged a look. Jimmy racked the shotgun.

"Didn't you learn your lesson the first time?" the security guard asked.

Emmett frowned, not liking any of this.

"Say that again," dared Emmett.

"I'll say that and more," said the security guard. "I'll say that you're a worthless no-good pile of shit. And I'll say you shoulda learned your lesson when you and your dumbass brothers got all shot to hell back in '92."

"Shut your mouth," demanded Emmett.

But the security guard kept right on yammering. "You're gonna foul this all up again. You couldn't do it forty years ago, and you can't do it now. You're just a hopeless screw up."

Emmett told the man to stand.

The security guard stood, not the least bit afraid of him.

Emmett turned the Colt on him.

"You stupid bastards shot a lot of good men that day," the security guard said. "I take pride in knowing that two of them slugs you took in your hide came from my gun, Emmett Dalton."

Emmett wasn't prepared for this. He hadn't planned to shoot anyone today.

Fuck it.

Examples had to be made.

"*You shot me?*" asked Emmett incredulously.

The security guard grinned big. "I shot your stupid ass twice."

Emmett looked down the barrel of the Colt at the security guard, still showing no fear. Emmett's finger tightened around the trigger.

This is it, he thought.

This man had to go.

Watching the man's face with the hopes of seeing his smug expression change, Emmett squeezed the trigger.

Click!

He squeezed it again.

Click!

Emmett stomped his foot. "*Goddammit*," he said.

"What is it?" asked Jimmy.

"I need to borrow your Peacemaker."

"Why?"

The security guard laughed heartily. "Because this stupid sumbitch forgot to load his goddamn pistol!"

Emmett heard a smattering of laughter around the room.

He slid the gun back into its holster.

Jimmy pulled out the Peacekeeper and tossed it to him. Emmett caught it and pointed it at the security guard.

"Not so funny now, is it?" he asked.

The security guard just kept grinning. "Nah," he said. "It's still pretty damned funny."

Emmett squeezed the trigger.

Blam!

The volley struck the security guard in his left eye, and the man and that stupid smile of his were no more.

Emmett and Jimmy ushered everyone into the vault and locked them inside.

The two bank robbers had gotten out of the First National Bank and made their way back to the Model A without a hitch. The street was still empty and there was nary a soul around. There were no police sirens blaring in the distance. In fact, it was dead silent. Emmett stomped on the gas and the automobile roared off down the street.

"Sorry about that," said Emmett. "I didn't want to shoot nobody."

"No problem. If he'd kept his damn fool mouth shut, he'd still be alive."

This made Emmett feel better.

"We gotta get this car off the street for a little while," he said.

Jimmy pointed. "There's a movie theater. Pull in there in the back lot."

And the two men went inside and watched *King Kong*, and no one ever showed up at the theater looking for them.

They had gotten away with it.

FOUR
THE WHEELMAN

ON THE HOUR-AND-A-HALF drive from Coffeyville to Joplin, Emmett and Jimmy discussed the robbery they'd just pulled. The two of them were like enthusiastic schoolchildren as they recounted it all.

"I didn't even have to tell the bank manager what to do," said Emmett. "He already knew."

Jimmy sat, smoking his pipe. "Sorry bastard didn't wanna join that security guard. Yeah, he knew what to do. That's the thing with these little banks in the Midwest; they been hit so many times most of 'em won't even put up a fight. They just hand the money over. The Barrows Gang and all them other robbers just made our job a little bit easier."

"Hell, even robbing banks has changed," observed Emmett. "I ain't never seen a bank manager just go for the vault without being asked. Back in the day, those bank managers acted like the damn money was theirs. A lot of 'em woulda died for money that didn't even belong to them."

"We were young at the wrong time. Just imagine if we were young right now. We'd be knocking 'em dead," said Jimmy.

Emmett stared down the road, finally saying, "Hell, we're gonna do that anyway, Jimmy. We're gonna show 'em all what a gang of old codgers can do. By God, they're gonna know our names."

"Everyone already knows your name," said McDaniel.

Emmett smiled, momentarily basking in his fame. "Well, if they didn't know us by now, they're damn sure gonna."

"I got a question."

"What is it?" asked Emmett.

"I'm not complaining or nothin' like that," said Jimmy. "But why are we the Emmett Dalton Gang and not the Jimmy McDaniels Gang?"

"On account of it being my idea. Besides, and I mean absolutely no offense here, my name is more famous than yours," said Emmett. "And I did tell 'em your name, too. I said we was Emmett Dalton and Jimmy McDaniels."

"I know. Again, I ain't complainin'. I was just wonderin', was all."

"Don't worry. I promise we're gonna make you famous, Jimmy. You and me, we're gonna be the next Barrows Gang, the next Dillinger... We're gonna own this world one of these days."

Emmett drove on, puffing on a big, fat cigar.

"We're almost to Joplin," said Emmett. "Where does your friend Tom Pickett live?"

JIMMY EXPLAINED the situation to Emmett—Tom was a broken-down old man, living in a rest home. He was suffering from emphysema, and he wasn't doing all that well.

"He lives in a damned rest home?" asked Emmett, irritated. "You could have mentioned this detail earlier."

"I wasn't sure you'd go along with it," said Jimmy. "But we gotta spring the man. He doesn't wanna be there anymore. He wants the same thing we want—to go out with a bang... To rob banks again. He wants to be an outlaw again."

Emmett chomped on his cigar. "Is there anything else I need to know about Tom Pickett?"

"Well," said Jimmy sheepishly, "I might have forgot to mention one other detail."

Emmett turned and looked at his partner. "What?"

"He's in a wheelchair."

Emmett sat upright. *"What?"*

"I suppose I shoulda mentioned that sooner."

"Yes," said Emmett. "I suppose you should have."

"I promised the man I'd get him out of there. We owe it to him."

"I don't owe the man shit. Hell, I don't even know him."

"But he was one of us," explained Jimmy. "He was an outlaw. That life he's livin' in that rest home, that ain't no kind of life at all. We gotta do this."

"If I was to help you get Tom out of the rest home, how the hell is he supposed to help us rob banks in a damned wheelchair?"

Jimmy shrugged. "I didn't think it would be a big deal. After all, he's just gonna be the wheelman."

Emmett laughed.

"What is it?"

"When you originally referred to him as the wheelman," said Emmett, "you forgot to mention the man actually comes with his own wheels."

Jimmy smiled. "Are we gonna break Tom Pickett out of that rest home, or what?"

"How's he gonna do security?" asked Emmett. "Third man, he usually pulls security outside the bank. Can your man do that?"

"I reckon he could. We'll just park right out front and give him a pistol. Then, he sees anybody coming, he can shoot 'em or fire off a round to let us know."

Emmett looked down for a moment, considering the matter. "Ah, what the hell," he said. "Let's do it."

"Really?"

"Sure. I wouldn't wanna live like that either. Let's go get the poor bastard out of there."

SUNNYVALE REST HOME was the kind of place that featured all the amenities of home without actually feeling anything even remotely like home. The place was overly sanitized and had the feel of a hospital more than a home. The rest home's advertisements touted it as a place to begin a new life, but the truth was apparent the moment Emmett and Jimmy walked in —this was a place where people went to die.

Emmett passed a pretty young nurse as he walked in. He smiled at her, and she gave him a sideways glance. "Hello," he said, stopping her. "Could you tell me where a patient named Tom Pickett might be staying?"

The pretty young thing smiled back, but Emmett didn't know if it was because of his good looks or that he reminded her of her own grandfather. "Sure thing. You just go straight down this hall to the front desk. They'll get you fellas signed in and then you can see Mr. Pickett. How does that sound?"

Emmett told her that sounded fine with him, and the two men proceeded down the hall to the front desk. When they came to the desk, no one was there. They waited for a few minutes, and finally a man approached them. "How can I help you?" he asked.

"We're old friends of Tom Pickett's," said Jimmy. "We're here to see him."

"Too bad you fellas just missed his birthday," the man said.

"It was a shame—no one came to visit." The man picked up a pencil and opened a notebook. "What are your names?"

"My name is John Smith," said Emmett. "And this handsome young devil here is Joe Johnson."

The man raised his face, looking them over. The crap aliases were probably a dead giveaway, but hell, Emmett had been forced to come up with them on the spur of the moment.

"Could you guys sign here?" asked the man, handing them the notebook.

Emmett signed in, handing the notebook to Jimmy. The second outlaw turned and whispered to Emmett, "What's my name again?"

Emmett whispered back, "Joe Johnson."

Jimmy scrawled the name. He then handed the notebook back to the man.

"Mr. Pickett is in room 105," said the man, pointing down the hall. "It's just three doors down on your left."

Emmett looked down the hall, then back at the man. "We just go on down?"

"Sure."

Emmett and Jimmy walked down the hallway, the place smelling simultaneously of disinfectant and death. When they got to Tom's room, Jimmy led the way seeing as how he knew the man.

Jimmy knocked.

Tom was a frail little man with paper-thin flesh draped over a pile of bones. He had liver spots all over his body. Jimmy had been right—Tom was on his last leg, so to speak. He looked bad. He turned his wheelchair to face them.

"Who is it?" asked Tom.

This was a bad start.

"It's me, Jimmy McDaniels."

"I didn't recognize you, Jimmy. How are you?"

Jimmy said, "I'm fine. How the hell are you?"

"Terrible," said Tom. "The bastards won't let me smoke in here. Can you believe that?"

"That's terrible," said Emmett, still puffing on his cigar.

"And who are you?" Tom asked Emmett.

Emmett extended his hand, and Jimmy introduced them. Tom shook his hand.

"Emmett Dalton?" he asked. "Are you the same Emmett Dalton that robbed those banks over in Coffeyville all those years ago?"

Emmett grinned. "I used to be."

"Well, it's damned fine to meet another old outlaw," said Tom, grinning a toothless grin. "What are you boys up to?"

"We're gonna spring you out this place," said Jimmy.

"You mean it?'

"Yeah."

Tom put his hand over his heart. "Thank you, sweet Jesus," he said. "I been prayin' for this for a long, long time. This here is surely the answer to my prayers."

"Is there anything you need to take with you?" asked Emmett.

"No, they can burn it all," said Tom. "I just want a damn cigarette."

EMMETT AND JIMMY tried to walk out of the rest home with the man, but they were stopped as they attempted to leave. "Where you taking this man?" asked the heavy-set nurse.

"We're just going for a walk," said Emmett. "It's a lovely day outside."

The nurse frowned. "This is most irregular. The residents can only go outside if they're accompanied by one of our staff members."

Emmett was already tired of this bullshit.

He reached into his jacket and pulled out his revolver, aiming it at the nurse. "We're gonna be leaving with this man, and there's not a damned thing you're gonna do about it."

The woman was visibly shaken.

She kept her mouth shut.

The two men wheeled Tom out to the Ford. Jimmy opened the coupe's door, and Emmett hefted Tom into the vehicle. "Damn, Tom, what the hell you been eatin'?" asked Emmett.

"He heavy?" asked Jimmy.

"Shit yes. He's like a sack of bricks."

Once Tom was in the backseat of the automobile, Jimmy folded up the wheelchair and stuffed it into the back beside him.

"Now what are we gonna do?" asked Tom.

Emmett smiled, looking at him in the rear-view mirror. "We're gonna rob us a few banks, Tom."

Tom lit up. "Then this really is the answer to all my prayers." Tom sat there silently for a moment before asking, "You don't think we're too old?"

"Hell no," said Emmett. "I think we're just fine."

"I'm gonna need a gun," said Tom.

Jimmy turned to him. "I brought you a Colt .45 revolver. That work for you?"

"Sounds great," said Tom. "There's just one more thing."

"Yeah?"

"How the hell am I supposed to be the getaway driver?"

Emmett looked in the mirror again. "What do you mean?"

Tom laughed. "I'm paralyzed from the waist down. How the hell am I supposed to drive a car?"

FIVE
MISERY IN MISSOURI

THE THREE OLD bank robbers checked into a place called the Hotel Connor. Emmett had originally planned to rob the Farmers Bank of Joplin just after breaking Tom Pickett out of the rest home, but he had reconsidered. Robbing two banks in one day would be an amazing thing, but that's what got him into trouble the first time around. No, there was no need to get cocky. Besides, they had a major problem. Their getaway driver couldn't use his legs, so how in the hell was he supposed to drive? Sure, Emmett and Jimmy had pulled the Coffeyville job alone, but that wouldn't really work more than once or twice. Jimmy had been right—they needed a third man.

And they had one—kind of.

But he was paralyzed.

What the hell have I gotten myself into here? Emmett asked himself. But being the good sport that he was, Emmett decided to make do with what they had. He decided to adapt to the situation. He went down to the lumber yard he'd passed on the way into town and purchased a single two-by-four. He then brought it back to the hotel.

"What the hell's that for?" asked Jimmy.

"This here is how Tom's gonna drive for us," said Emmett proudly.

Tom, choking on a cigarette, asked, "How?'

Emmett held up the two-by-four. "You can hit the accelerator with this. That allows you to use your arms. Then you don't have to worry about your legs. What do you think?"

"I think you're crazy," said Tom. "That's what I think."

The man wasn't joking.

"What makes you say that?"

"What the hell kind of gang would want a crippled getaway driver?" asked Tom. "That shit don't make sense."

Emmett had to admit that the whole thing did sound crazy, especially when you said it out loud. But Emmett was as loyal as the day was long, and besides, they were in desperate need of a third man, and it wasn't like they could just go and run an ad in the *Joplin Globe*.

So, they were stuck with old Tom Pickett.

"Should we plan out the robbery?" asked Jimmy.

"What's to plan?" asked Emmett. "We'll check the place out in the morning before we pull the job, just to make sure everything looks good. You know how it is—we just go in there, guns blazing, and rob the damn place. It don't take a lot of leg work. Besides, this is Joplin. This is the Farmers Bank. Remember, they been hit three or four times already this year. Like you said, easy-peezy."

Jimmy nodded, puffing on his pipe. "What do you wanna do now?"

"I figure we'll go and get some dinner, maybe go to another show."

"Another show?"

"Sure," said Emmett. "We'll get our minds off the thing. I

mean, it's not like we have anything to worry about anyway. This is Joplin. What could go wrong?"

EMMETT DIDN'T LIKE the way the day was starting. Today's issue of the *Globe* had come out, and they'd done a write-up on the Coffeyville robbery. The article didn't sit well with Emmett one damn bit. In the article the reporter referred to them as "the Old Timers Gang" instead of the Emmett Dalton Gang. Apparently, the Coffeyville Police had given them this mocking moniker, and the media seemed to be eating it up.

"Goddammit," Emmett muttered, rereading the article for the third time. "We can't have this. This is bullshit. How are we gonna get respect if we can't even get the bastards to call us by our rightful name?"

Emmett decided he would telephone the editor of the *Joplin Globe* and personally inform him of his mistake. Maybe, just maybe, the damage to the gang's collective reputation could still be salvaged.

"I need to talk to the editor," said Emmett, using the telephone in the hotel hallway. "I need to know, what's that sumbitches' name?"

The woman on the other end of the phone said politely, "Alvin Cobb is the editor. Hold on and I'll get him for you."

Emmett put his hand over the receiver and turned to Jimmy, standing behind him, smoking his pipe. "She's going to get him now." He then turned back to the telephone and waited for Alvin Cobb. A moment later, Cobb picked up the telephone.

"Hello, this is Alvin Cobb," the man said. The second Emmett heard his voice he immediately pictured Cobb as a portly, well-dressed, arrogant prick.

Emmett raised his mouth to the telephone, a cigar in his

mouth. "My name is Emmett Dalton. I robbed that bank in Coffeyville yesterday."

"Is this really Emmett Dalton?"

"Yes, sir, it sure is," said Emmett.

"What can I do for you, Mr. Dalton?"

"I just called to tell you that your facts were all wrong in that story you did in the paper this morning."

"Oh?" asked Cobb. "How so?"

"Your paper called us the Old Timers Gang, and that ain't our proper name."

"Is that right?" asked Cobb, a lightness in his voice suggesting he was trying not to laugh.

This irritated Emmett. "We're the Emmett Dalton Gang."

"Surely you must know every newspaper in the country is now calling you the Old Timers Gang. I'm afraid the damage has already been done, Mr. Dalton. Now everyone's gonna call you the Old Timers Gang from here on. You might as well get used to it."

"Hell's bells," muttered Emmett.

"Can I interview you while I have you on the telephone?"

Emmett looked at Jimmy. He wasn't sure this was a good idea. He put his hand over the receiver and asked Jimmy what he should do. "Tell the man yes," said Jimmy. Emmett figured what the hell and agreed to be interviewed.

"You're an author and a motion picture actor now, Mr. Dalton," said Cobb. "What made you decide to pick up where you left off and start robbing banks again?"

So, Emmett told him the truth. "Other than John Dillinger, these younger bank robbers got it all wrong. They got no style. They tote around those big goddamn Tommy Guns, shooting up the place. Where's the grace in that? Where's the style?"

"I got you. No style," repeated Cobb. "So, what made you decide to rob the First National Bank of Coffeyville again?"

"I figured where's a better place to start than where I left off," said Emmett. "And I felt like I had a score to settle with Coffeyville. Last time we was there, they shot and killed my brothers. The sons of bitches shot me full of holes, and I spent fourteen years behind bars for that robbery."

"So, this was payback?"

"You're damn right this was payback. The name Emmett Dalton is a name those sons of bitches aren't likely to forget any time soon, I'll tell you that."

Cobb said, "I'm sure you're right, Mr. Dalton. When you were in that bank, you shot and killed a man. Hold on. I'll have to look it up..." Cobb got quiet for a minute before returning. "A Mr. Jeb Murtree, a bank security guard. What do you have to say about that?"

"I ain't got much to say about it," explained Emmett. "If the damn fool had kept his stupid mouth shut, he'd still be alive today. But no, he had to go runnin' off at the mouth. He had to talk shit. Well, look where that got him."

"May I inquire as to where you are currently?" asked Cobb.

Emmett rubbed his moustache. "No comment."

"Are you in Joplin?"

Emmett stared at the telephone, not knowing what to say.

Shit. This was a mistake.

"Mr. Dalton?" asked Cobb.

Unsure what to do to cover his tracks, Emmett hung up the phone. He turned to Jimmy. "Come on," he said. "We gotta move fast if we're gonna rob that bank. That son of a bitch knows we're in Joplin. I guarantee you he's gonna call the cops."

"And we're gonna rob the bank anyway?"

"Yup."

"Right now?"

"Right goddamn now," said Emmett. "Help me get Tom's

wheelchair down the stairs, so we can get him propped up behind the steering wheel."

"We're gonna go and rob the Farmers Bank without doing any leg work?" asked Jimmy. "That sounds like a bad fucking idea."

"We'll be fine."

Seven minutes later Tom Pickett pulled the Model A right up in front of the bank. It was just after nine.

"I got a bad feeling about this," said Tom.

"Yeah," said Jimmy. "Me too."

This got Emmett steamed. He held up his Colt. "Are you bastards backing out on me? 'Cause I'll rob this goddamn bank all by my lonesome if I have to."

"Of course not," said Jimmy. "Let's do it."

"Am I still the leader of this gang?" asked Emmett.

"We ain't got time for dick measuring," said Tom, smoking his cigarette. "You dummies got to get in there now if we're gonna rob this fucker."

The man had a point.

When Emmett and Jimmy entered the bank, there were no customers in the place. It was just the bank employees.

The bank manager—a little redheaded fella—spoke up. "The police just telephoned," he said. "They're on their way now. If I were you boys, I'd get out of here while you still can. Here in a few minutes this place is gonna be crawlin' with cops."

Emmett was nervous. He looked back at Jimmy, who just shrugged.

"Get down on the ground," said Emmett. "Anybody moves or hits the alarm, they die. You get it?"

Nobody said a word.

Emmett ordered the bank manager to fill a couple of bags with cash from the drawers. This time Emmett figured he'd just skip the vault what with the cops coming and all. The bank manager agreed, and he leaned forward to get the bags. When he came back up, Emmett saw at once that he didn't have a bag in his hand—he had a pistol.

Goddammit, Emmett thought.

Emmett didn't want to kill anyone, but he had no choice.

He was on autopilot now, those old senses coming back to him.

He fired the .40-44 caliber, shooting the bank manager in the Adam's apple. The manager dropped the pistol and reached for his throat, blood seeping out between his fingers. The man was all wigglin' around, on the verge of convulsing.

Emmett put him out of his misery.

This time he shot him in the cheek, killing him instantly. The bank manager's eyes rolled back in his head, and he crumpled to the floor.

Jimmy yelled, "Come on, let's get out of here!"

Emmett knew there was no time. He couldn't hear sirens yet, but he knew damn well they were coming. "Stay on the floor," he yelled. "Anybody gets up, they die!"

And he turned for the door.

THE THREE BANK robbers were now speeding away in the coupe. They passed a couple of police cars going in the opposite direction.

"What the hell kind of robbers are you guys?" asked Tom.

"You weren't there," said Emmett. "It got ugly fast."

"So let me get this straight," Tom said. "You shot and killed a man and then got out of there without so much as a goddamn dollar? What kind of bullshit half-assed gang is this, Emmett?"

Emmett was pissed. "Just shut up and smoke your damn cigarette, pops."

SIX
GOOD AND LOYAL SERVANTS

WANTING to put as much road between themselves and the Joplin robbery, Emmett and the gang headed down US 54 to St. Louis. The air was turning colder. Halloween was about a week away, and the wind had picked up tremendously. It looked as though it might snow at any moment.

Emmett and Jimmy had scouted the bank while Tom stayed back in the room and read through the Bible as he was trying to become better friends with God "on account of how we might be seeing him soon." This irked Emmett a bit. Not just that Tom was implying they might be shot and killed any day, but also that he now talked about nothing else but God. The thing that made such conversations with Tom interesting was that he always laced each sentence about Christianity with profanity of some sort. His heart was in the right place, but he wasn't the brightest guy who ever robbed a bank. He'd say things like, "Jesus Christ was one tough son of a bitch" or ask if anyone knew how big "Noah's goddamn ark" was. Emmett had nothing against religion. Hell, he'd been raised in church and had married Julia, a good God-fearing woman who had dragged his ass into church each week. But Tom wanted to talk about God all the time. He seemed to know no other subject.

So, when they walked into the hotel room in St. Louis and were confronted by Tom about their lack of "goddamn religion," they weren't really all that surprised.

"I been thinkin'," said Tom, taking a drag from his cigarette. "It's high time you boys found our Lord Jesus Christ. Now I know both of you been to church a time or two, but you need to really study the Bible and pray more. That might help us to be better goddamn bank robbers. You know, if God is on our side, then who can be against us?"

Emmett asked, "You think a fella could really pray to God about things like committin' robberies?"

"Why, sure I do," said Tom. "Jesus helps with all things, even some things that ain't so good. Besides, all we're doing is takin' money away from the rich people. That ain't so bad. In a way, we're doing a good thing. You know what the Bible says about the rich man? It says a camel would have an easier time passing through the hole in a goddamn needle than a rich bastard would have of getting' into heaven."

Emmett nodded. It made sense.

Jimmy said, "Maybe we should start prayin' before every job we do."

"That's exactly what I was thinking," said Tom. "It's like God went into your mind and filled you with the same thought he filled my head with."

THE NEXT DAY they were sitting idly in the Ford, right there in the middle of the street. Automobiles were passing by them and tooting their horns, but they didn't pay them any mind at all. They were in the middle of prayer.

"Dear God, our Lord Jesus Christ we speak unto you," said

Tom, leading the thing. "We look to you and ask as your humble goddamn servants that you come down off of your seat up there in heaven and watch over us as we rob this place. Please don't let none of these stupid sons of bitches try anything in here, and don't make Emmett and Jimmy have to kill anybody, oh God, oh wise one. We promise that, aside from robbin' banks and occasionally killin' folks, to be good and loyal servants. We are your sheep, and you are our—"

This was when the prayer was interrupted by a knock on the window.

The three bank robbers opened their eyes and looked up, seeing the cop standing there. Emmett rolled the window down.

"You boys can't park here," said the cop. "You're stopping the flow of traffic."

It was at this point the cop saw the pistols and the sawed-off Greener. He stepped back and reached for his gun. "What are you boys doing here with all these guns?"This time it was Tom that acted. He raised the short barrel of the coach gun past Emmett's head and squeezed the trigger, blasting the cop back a good foot. Lucky for them there were no pedestrians around. Emmett jumped out of the automobile and dragged the cop's bloody body back into the coupe.

"Ah, Jesus Christ," he muttered.

"What?" asked Tom.

"My upholstery," said Emmett. "I'm gonna get blood all over it." He paused for a moment before adding, "Stupid goddamn cop."

Jimmy looked at Tom. Emmett was still standing half in and half out the automobile door, and the dead cop was sitting up in the seat between he and Tom.

"Let's hurry up and finish our prayer," said Tom.

And so, they did.

135

. . .

EMMETT AND JIMMY walked into the bank, business as usual, and they felt they were right back in the swing of robbing banks. It had all come back to them just as it's said about riding a bike. Their pistols were down beside them, and they were wearing long coats. The place was packed.

Nobody noticed them at first.

Everyone just went about their business.

And then someone screamed out, "He's got a gun!" People started freaking out, turning, screaming and holding their children.

"Everyone get down on the damned floor!" screamed Emmett. "Anybody moves and we start shooting. We're the Emmett Dalton Gang. Maybe you heard of us. Well, we're here to rob this here bank today. Anybody got any questions?"

There were none.

Jimmy covered the front doors as Emmett stalked towards the front counter. "I should mention that if anybody trips the alarm, we're gonna start killing folks," said Emmett to the teller. "Now kindly start sacking up all the bills in those drawers." He turned towards a man still standing, obviously the bank manager, ready to go down with his proverbial ship.

"You," said Emmett. "You the manager?"

"Yes," said the man nervously.

"Let's go open your vault." Emmett walked around the counter towards the bank manager, but the man didn't move an inch.

"I won't do it," said the bank manager.

"Yes, you will," said Emmett. "Or else my little gun makes a big noise, if you catch my drift."

"I do, but I won't do it."

Emmett turned and shot a man lying on the floor in the head, his brains and blood spraying a good foot away from him.

"Let's try this again," said Emmett.

"No, I still won't do it."

Emmett turned and shot a bank teller, and then looked back at the bank manager.

"I still won't do it," said the bank manager.

This was when Emmett heard a woman's voice say, "Oh, Jesus Christ, Charlie."

Emmett turned and saw a woman—a bank employee—coming towards them. Before he could swivel his pistol, she said, "To hell with you, Charlie. I'll open the goddamn safe."

The bank manager looked disgusted by all this. Emmett raised the pistol and shot the man. "We don't need you anymore, Charlie," he said. He followed the woman to the vault. She turned the dial a few times and the safe came open.

"The money's already bagged up in there," said the woman. "Just grab it and go."

Emmett took two steps into the vault before he realized what he'd done. The woman closed the door on him, locking him inside.

"*Open this goddamn door right now!*" screamed Emmett, but no one came.

Shit, he thought. *What am I gonna do now?*

Emmett Dalton's comeback wasn't turning out quite the way he'd envisioned it.

Emmett sat inside the vault in darkness for about five minutes before he heard gunshots outside. He'd be damned if it didn't sound like sub-machine gun chatter. Then he heard the dial of the vault again, and the door opened.

There was a man standing there, dressed in a fancy suit, carrying a Tommy gun.

"Come on out of there," he said.

Emmett started to walk out, but the man said, "Don't forget the money."

He went back and grabbed the two bags of bills that were inside the vault and then walked out.

"We can shake hands later," said the man, smoking a big, fat cigar. "My name's George Nelson. Everybody calls me Baby Face."

"Pleased to make your acquaintance, Mr. Nelson," said Emmett.

Baby Face chuckled. "I'm sure you are."

Emmett looked around and saw that there were two more robbers, along with his pal Jimmy. The rest of the robbery went without a hitch until they were leaving the bank. As they were walking out, Baby Face sprayed into the crowd with his Tommy gun, wounding and killing a handful of people. It was, as Emmett would later recount, the most gruesome thing he'd ever witnessed.

Emmett was still carrying the money when they got outside.

"You go ahead and carry that," said Baby Face. "Just follow me. I'll be in that Studebaker right in front of you boys."

THE THREE MEMBERS of the Emmett Dalton Gang followed Baby Face and his boys to a rundown shack about thirty miles outside St. Louis. Once they were all inside, Baby Face introduced them to the other three members of his gang. They were: Homer Van Meter, Tommy Carroll, and Eddie Green. Then Baby Face said, "And boys, these are the members of the Old Timers Gang."

The band of outlaws looked as though they were genuinely impressed.

Emmett was not.

"We don't go by that name, the Old Timers Gang," said Emmett. "We're the Emmett Dalton Gang."

Baby Face put out his hand for Emmett to shake, and Emmett did so. "Pleased to make your acquaintance."

Baby Face smiled. "Likewise, Mr. Dalton."

"So, what do we do about the money, since we both sort of robbed that bank?" asked Jimmy.

"We'll split it, fifty-fifty," said Baby Face. "After all, we got nothin' but respect for you old guys."

The feeling was not mutual. Although Emmett was glad Baby Face came along and saved his ass, he was not particularly pleased about his having shot a handful of innocent people. Sure, Emmett shot people when he needed to, but this was something else; this was a fucking bloodbath, and Emmett wanted no part of it.

But what was done was done, and there wasn't a goddamn thing Emmett could do to change any of it.

SEVEN
MEETING DILLINGER

"Why don't we just go ahead and divide up the money now," said Emmett, lighting his cigar. "Then we'll be on our merry way."

"Don't worry about it," said Baby Face. "We can divide up the money in a bit. For now, why don't you boys kick back and relax. There's someone comin' that I want you to meet. I know he'll want to meet you."

This made Emmett uncomfortable. He liked being in control; he liked knowing what was happening. "What do you mean you want us to meet someone? Who?"

Baby Face said, "Relax, it ain't a trap or nothin'. We all look up to you older guys. I wouldn't set you up or nothin'. It ain't like I'm gonna be workin' with the Feds... I just robbed a bank today, and on top of that I done killed more of their FBI men than anyone in U.S. history, so I ain't no friend of Melvin Purvis and his goddamn G-Men."

"I wasn't thinkin' that," said Emmett. "I just don't like being in the dark here. I wanna know who I'm meeting."

"This guy's a bank robber like us. A real big fan of yours.

Hell, we all feel the same way. I hope I'm still as spry and as crazy as you sons of bitches are when I'm your age."

Emmett enjoyed being complimented; it was nice hearing these things from a fellow bank robber with as much notoriety as Baby Face Nelson had.

"So, are you gonna tell me who we're meeting with, or not?" asked Emmett.

"Fine," said Baby Face. "I wanted it to be a surprise."

Emmett said nothing. He just puffed on that big old cigar of his.

Baby Face said, "His name's John Dillinger. Maybe you heard of him? He's gonna be here for a day. He uses this hideout sometimes, too."

EMMETT AND JIMMY sat and played cards with Baby Face and his boys. Tom mostly just sat in his wheelchair and smoked his cigarettes, telling everyone about the impending return of Jesus Christ. Nobody much wanted to hear about it, but everyone got a real kick out of hearing him curse as he did it. He was telling everyone a story about "that motherfucker Moses" when Eddie came in and said, "Dillinger's here."

Baby Face sat down his cards. "He just got here?"

"Yeah," said Eddie. "He's parking the car around back now."

Everyone stood up to greet him. A couple minutes later, Dillinger entered the room. He was as dapper and charismatic as Clark Gable, only more handsome, and with smaller ears. This was a man who could have been anything he'd wanted to be, and all he wanted was to be a bank robber. Emmett respected a man who had respect for the craft.

At first Dillinger didn't see Emmett and the boys standing there. He came in, hugged Baby Face, and said his hellos to

Baby Face's crew. When he looked up and saw Emmett standing there, his expression was one of genuine awe. "Holy shit," he said. "You're Emmett Dalton."

Dillinger put out his hand for Emmett to shake, and Emmett did.

"You've said an awful lot of nice things about me in the papers," said Dillinger. "And I want you to know, I have a mutual respect for you old boys. You fellas been at this for a long, long time, and I just respect the hell out of that."

Before long, everyone had gone back to playing cards. Emmett and Dillinger sat facing each other, away from the card game, trading stories of past robberies.

"What kind of advice could you give a young buck like me?" asked Dillinger.

"I'm not as sharp at this shit as I used to be," said Emmett, "so I don't really know that I'm one to give advice. But I will say this—you shouldn't be using that Tommy gun to shoot everybody up."

"I shouldn't?" asked Dillinger, smoking a cigarette.

"No, and I'll tell you why. You're too good for that. You're too classy for that. No offense intended to our present company, but the Thompson sub-machine gun is a classless weapon. Sure, it's handy in a wartime situation, but to take it into a bank and shoot the place up? It just reeks of classless amateurism."

Dillinger glanced over at Baby Face, lost in his card game. "Baby Face loves to shoot people," said Dillinger. "I don't much care for killing folks, but I've had to do it on occasion."

"Me too," said Emmett, puffing on his cigar. "But I always use a revolver. It's a more noble, more respectable weapon."

"I suppose you're right," said Dillinger, nodding. "Speaking of revolvers, I was wondering something: did you ever have a showdown with anybody back in the day? You know, one of those duels out in the dusty street like they always have on those cowboy radio shows."

"Nah, nothing like that," said Emmett, chuckling. "But I did have a second cousin, Lester, who got involved in one of those."

"What happened?"

"Lester ended up out in the graveyard," said Emmett. "The son of a bitch that shot him put a hole right through his eye. They had to have a closed-casket funeral. I never did like that much, seein' as how Lester was kind of soft in the head anyway. It ain't right for a fella to shoot a man who ain't right in his head, you know?"

Dillinger nodded in agreement, hanging on Emmett's every word.

"Now I got a question for you," said Emmett.

"Okay," said Dillinger. "What is it?"

"'That story about your escapin' from the hoosegow with a gun made from a bar of soap—is that true?"

"Nah," said Dillinger. "It was actually a gun made of wood. Soap's a better story though."

"Still a neat trick."

"Thanks," said Dillinger. "Is it true you got shot more than twenty times when you and your brothers tried to rob them banks out in Kansas?"

"Yes, sir, it is. I took twenty-three bullets."

"And you lived. How remarkable."

"You boys," said Emmett. "You're a lot like we were. The 1890s and the 1930s ain't a whole lot different if you think about it. You guys are out here robbin' banks, same as we were. The only difference now is the technology. You boys got fancier guns and you get to drive away in an automobile instead of on horseback."

Dillinger, still looking at Emmett with admiration, asked, "Do you ever miss those old days?"

"Every fucking day," said Emmett.

"What do you miss most?"

"I know this is gonna sound silly comin' from an old bank robber like me, but it seems to me that people used to have more respect for one another. People said things like 'please' and 'thank you.' You ask me about things changin', where the hell do I begin? There's been so many big changes in these past forty years or so I can hardly keep up."

"I'm sure," said Dillinger. "I'll bet those Gatling guns were really something to deal with back in the day."

"Those were like our Thompson sub-machine guns," Emmett said. "Except you couldn't carry those sumbitches around with you. They had to sit on a tripod, but if you came face to face with one of those—like the Wild Bunch—you were deader than hell."

Dillinger said, "I love hearing these old stories, Emmett. You boys are really something. What the hell made you want to go back out there and rob banks again? Hell, it looked like you had it all—steady income, legendary status, pretty wife... Why'd you do it, Emmett?"

"Maybe I'm just too stupid to know any better," said Emmett, a big grin on his face.

"I'm serious."

"Well, I just missed it," said Emmett. "There ain't nothin' in this world like that thrill you get when you run into a bank with your gun out and you tell all those people what to do. There's nothing like that sense of control... It's just an incredible rush that's unlike anything I've experienced doing anything else. People used to say, Emmett, you've made it—you're a movie actor. People think that's the pinnacle of the thing, but the truth is, it ain't nowhere as fun as robbin' those banks was."

Dillinger nodded in agreement. "I know exactly what you mean. Hell, I've already made enough money to retire from this game, but it's in my blood now."

"Right," said Emmett.

"It's there, and it don't leave. You know, I even have dreams about robbing banks when I go to sleep at night. I tell you, that kind of thing makes my pecker harder than a pretty woman."

Emmett chuckled. He knew exactly what Dillinger meant. He felt exactly the same way.

EIGHT
MELVIN PURVIS TAKES A STAND

FBI SPECIAL AGENT Melvin Purvis was just a regular guy, just like anyone else. Sure, the newspapers made him out to be some larger-than-life crime-buster, but he was just a normal blue-collar working man. One time a newspaper reporter had asked Melvin, "What makes you tick?" To this, Melvin had replied, "I love my job." And he did. Not because it made him feel powerful or because it gave him the sense of control robbing banks gave Emmett Dalton. No, he just loved doing something he was good at.

And he *was* good.

He was the best when it came to apprehending the nation's most wanted robbers and killers.

His boss at the Federal Bureau of Investigations, J. Edgar Hoover, wasn't his biggest fan, and Melvin had no idea as to why. He sensed it was because Hoover wanted all the recognition and glory Melvin was getting. And Melvin really couldn't understand such a thought, considering he himself hated that particular aspect of his job. He wasn't a particularly gifted speaker, so he loathed talking to the press. And when people told him their children looked up to him as a hero, he only shook his head in dismay.

He was no hero.

Babe Ruth was a hero.

Franklin D. Roosevelt was a hero.

But Melvin Purvis was just a regular man who happened to be very good at his job. End of story.

Today word had come down directly through Hoover that Purvis was to now move the Emmett Dalton Gang up into the FBI's top ten most wanted list, as they had only yesterday been responsible for a handful of deaths in a bank robbery down in St. Louis.

"Geez, how old are those guys?" Purvis had asked.

"Age hasn't got shit to do with it, Purvis," said Hoover. "Those rotten S.O.B.s are running around in cahoots with Baby Face Nelson, which makes them just as deadly as he is. These are men who kill with no remorse, and who rob whatever they can get their greedy little hands on. They must be stopped at once. Surely you can accomplish this, Purvis. As you said, they're old men."

Melvin hated when Hoover talked to him like that. Hoover always spoke with disdain and a holier-than-thou haughtiness Melvin couldn't abide. Here he was, out here doing everything in his power to accomplish every goal Hoover set out for him, and Hoover showed no appreciation whatsoever.

Fuck Hoover.

Melvin didn't do this because he wanted to please his boss.

He did it because he loved his job.

It was three o'clock in the afternoon when they held the press conference. There were a good twenty-five reporters in attendance, all of them there to hear what Melvin Purvis had to say.

"Today we're here to announce that we're adding the bank robbers known as the Emmett Dalton Gang, a.k.a. the Old Timers Gang, to the FBI's most wanted list," explained Purvis into the microphone. "We will begin a manhunt at once to apprehend these cold-blooded killers, who just this week were responsible, or at least partly responsible, for the deaths of nearly twenty people in a bank robbery down in St. Louis, Missouri."

"How old are those guys?" asked one reporter.

"It is true that these men are older," said Purvis, "but age has nothing to do with this. Certain privileges come with advanced age, but the right to rob and kill people is not one of them."

Another reporter spoke up. "Will there be a reward set for these men?"

"There will be a reward for any information leading to the arrest of these fellas," explained Purvis. "The amount has yet to be determined, but it will be substantial."

"Are these the oldest men ever to be put on the FBI's most wanted list?"

Purvis smiled. "I think that's safe to say." Everyone in the room laughed.

"How many murders are these men responsible for?" someone asked.

"We figure them for about twenty-five murders," explained Purvis.

"And how many robberies have they committed so far?"

"They've committed at least four robberies."

"How can you be sure you'll get them?" asked one reporter. "I mean, no offense, but you haven't been able to catch Baby Face Nelson or Dillinger or the Barrows Gang yet."

"We're very close to apprehending all these different groups," said Purvis. "Because of the secretive nature of our investigations, I can't really divulge much more than that at this time."

A reporter in the back asked, "How do you intend to catch these groups of killers and robbers?"

"We will ultimately win this war on crime," said Purvis, "through highly-sophisticated scientific techniques and superior leadership. The FBI will not stop hunting these groups of wanted felons until they are dead or in prison, I assure you that."

EMMETT WAS SITTING on the bed in a hotel in Chicago when he read about Melvin Purvis' declaring them as wanted fugitives on the FBI's most wanted list.

"Well, shit," he said. "At least they got our name right."

Jimmy sat in a chair, smoking his pipe. "I don't like it. This is serious. When the FBI gets involved, that's the big time. That's a whole 'nother animal there. Those G-Men don't stop coming, don't stop trying, until they catch their man. No, sir, I don't like it one bit."

Tom, enveloped in a cloud of cigarette smoke, said, "Maybe if somebody had kept his goddamn gun from going off, we wouldn't be in this predicament."

"What the hell is that supposed to mean?" asked Emmett.

"It meant maybe you should have kept your spurs from jingle-janglin' so much and tried not to shoot anybody and everybody that got in your way," said Tom. "I don't see Jimmy here blastin' up the place, shootin' motherfuckers willy-nilly. No, sir, that's just you. I only shot one sumbitch and that was because I had no other choice."

"I didn't shoot anybody I didn't have to shoot," said Emmett, becoming defensive.

"How about that security guard back there in Coffeyville?"

asked Tom. "Why'd you shoot him? Because of your pride? Because you couldn't let an old man talk a little shit without putting a goddamn hole in him?"

"I'm listening to you talk shit," said Emmett, "and I haven't shot you yet."

Tom just stared at him. "I suspect the day will come when you do."

"You know," said Emmett, "I resent this bullshit. It's not like I shot up all those people back there in St. Louis. That was Baby Face."

"And why'd he shoot 'em?" asked Tom. "Because your dumb ass got locked inside the vault. All of this is your fault. Do you see a recurring theme here, Emmett? Everything fucked up that happens is always your fault."

Emmett took a deep breath and tried to diffuse the situation. "Why don't you just smoke your cigarette and get some rest," said Emmett. "I'm sure everything will look a whole lot sunnier in the morning."

To this, Tom said, "Why don't you go fuck yourself?"

And that was that.

NINE
THE CHICAGO JOB

"There's lots of banks in Chicago," observed Emmett. "We should be able to find one and make a nice payday for ourselves."

"Where you figure we'll head after this?" asked Tom, smoking his millionth cigarette of the day.

"I dunno," said Emmett. "Maybe we'll take a vote."

When they reached Chicago, they drove around looking at all the banks, finally settling on one called the West Town State Bank. This decision wasn't based on anything more than Jimmy and Tom's saying it "felt right," but Emmett figured he'd let them have their way since they were starting to question his decisions.

After that, they went back to the Drake Hotel, where they were staying. Emmett parked the Model A in the lot beside the hotel. He and Jimmy then assisted Tom with getting out of the automobile and getting situated in his wheelchair.

"What do we do with the bags of money?" asked Jimmy.

"We'll leave 'em in the Ford," said Emmett.

Jimmy scratched his head, unsure about this. "You think

that's a good idea?'"I think it'll be just fine. We'll just push the bags down under the seats where they're out of sight. Besides, in a swanky place like this, no one's gonna be after our money."

As they were walking into the hotel, Jimmy asked Emmett, "What are you gonna do with your share of the money?" Emmett had no answer for it. "I already got money. Maybe I'll give it to the poor people. God knows with this depression on, there's enough of 'em out there."

"Piss on 'em," said Tom, rubbing his yellowing stubble. "Maybe they wouldn't be poor if they'd get off their asses and do something to fix their situation. That's what Jesus says."

"Jesus says 'piss on 'em'?" asked Emmett.

No response.

"Well, I'm gonna buy a new Stetson," said Jimmy. "One of them nice fedoras all the dapper dandies are wearin' now. How about you, Tom? What are you gonna buy?"

"I don't know that I need anything money could give me other than a little companionship with a pretty lady, and even then, I'm seventy-five fuckin' years old, so what good's that gonna do me?" He paused, thinking for a minute. "I don't reckon there's anything I really need that I don't already have."

THEY IDLED the car up in front of the West Town State Bank at just after ten. Tom was using the two-by-four to drive, with a sawed-off shotgun sitting between his legs. Emmett and Jimmy prepared to jump out, pistols in their hands.

Tom led the group in prayer. This time there were no interruptions.

"Alright, old man," said Emmett. "We'll be right back. You stay here and keep watch. You see anybody doing anything they shouldn't oughta be doin', you either blast 'em with this shotgun or fire off a round so we'll know something's goin' down. Got it?"

Tom looked annoyed. "This ain't my first trip to the rodeo, sonny."

Emmett looked at Jimmy. "I guess it's time."

The two men climbed out of the Ford, their pistols down at their sides. They managed to slip through the pedestrians on the street unnoticed, and soon they were entering the bank. There was an old security guard, probably about Emmett's age —*why were they all so damned old?*—sitting in a wooden chair to the right. Emmett pointed his pistol at the guard, and the guard did nothing; he just sat there. Once Jimmy was in the door and had the security guard covered, Emmett announced, "This is a goddamn robbery! Everybody get down on the ground now! Anybody don't do what they're supposed to be doin' catches a bullet, you got it?"

Everyone got down. There were only a handful of customers, all men and women, no children, in the place. There were approximately ten employees counting the security guard now lying on the floor by the door.

Emmett approached the counter. "Where's the bank manager?"

"Hello," said one of the men, smiling. "I'm Edward."

"You're the manager?"

"Yes, sir," said Edward.

"Okay, Ed, what I need you to do is to open that vault and get us as much money in bags as you can within a minute." Emmett turned around to address everyone else. "Anybody hits the alarm, Edward here buys the farm. Any questions?"

No questions.

Emmett came around the counter and walked to the vault with Edward, who was still smiling. He unlocked the old vault and pulled it open.

"You probably shouldn't be doing this, mister," said Edward.

"No shit," said Emmett. He waved his pistol at the man. "Get in there and get me my money."

Edward just grinned. "If you say so."

Edward entered the vault and bagged up the money. As he did so, Emmett turned and scanned the room. Everyone was doing exactly what they were supposed to be doing.

Now this is how you rob a goddamn bank, thought Emmett.

Emmett looked down at his watch and told Edward, "Time. Gimme what you got." Edward handed over three sacks of cash.

"Now what?" asked Edward.

"You stay here in the vault," said Emmett, closing the door on him. He then turned to the rest of the room. "You all just got robbed by the Emmett Dalton Gang. When the cops come and ask you who done this, you be sure and tell 'em that—the Emmett Dalton Gang, you got it?"

And Emmett and Jimmy went out the door. They ran through the pedestrian traffic on the sidewalk, carrying guns and bags of cash. No one paid them any mind whatsoever.

AFTER THE ROBBERY, Emmett and the boys went to the show and watched *Duck Soup*. Then they went out to eat at a place called the Triangle Restaurant. As they dined on celebratory T-bone steaks, they talked themselves up about the job they'd just pulled.

"I thought that went pretty well," said Jimmy.

"It seemed a little too easy," said Tom. "I dunno, just didn't feel right."

This pissed Emmett off as the entire reason they had robbed that particular bank had been because Tom and Jimmy thought it "just felt right." But now Tom was saying it felt wrong. Here Emmett had done a good deed in breaking Tom out of the rest home, and all Tom ever did was bitch and moan about anything and everything. Hell, he had even complained about the picture show they'd selected, saying Jesus Christ didn't like comedies.

Fuck Tom, Emmett thought. *Who gives a shit what he thinks?*

From now on, things were gonna be different. From now on, Emmett was gonna make it clear who the goddamn boss was around this place. This was his gang, and by God he wasn't about to take any crap off an old washed-up, never-was asshole like Tom Pickett.

"What do you mean it doesn't feel right?" asked Emmett.

"Didn't you notice how no one put up a fight?" asked Tom. "That ain't normal. They just stared at you and handed over the money."

Emmett felt himself getting short with Tom. "Look," he said, "we finally had a good robbery, and here you are complainin' about it. That ain't exactly normal either."

"I'm not complaining," said Tom. "I was just pointing out that it all seemed a little too easy. It made me feel funny, that's all."

Emmett was still annoyed. In fact, he wasn't really in the mood to be around either of the old men. Both of 'em acted like they knew every damn thing, and Emmett was still peeved at Jimmy for not telling him about all the baggage that came with Tom's grouchy, old, crippled ass. Although he had barely touched his steak and baked potato, Emmett dismissed himself from the table. "I'm gonna step outside and get some air," he said. "Have me a cigar."

Emmett stood up, folded his napkin, sat it over his plate, and walked out of the restaurant.

Jimmy looked at Tom. "Something's the matter with him."

"Well," said Tom. "He'd better get it corrected real fast, or else he's liable to get us all shot to hell in one of these piss-poorly-planned robberies of his."

"Agreed."

And that was all they said.

TEN

THE SYNDICATE

THE MORNING STARTED OUT SHITTY, and only managed to get worse from there. First, Emmett had gone down to the lobby to get a copy of the *Chicago Daily News*. The story about yesterday's bank robbery was splashed across the front page. The headline read: "OLD TIMERS GANG STRIKES AGAIN!" Right off the bat this irritated Emmett; the newspapers were still referring to them as the Old Timers Gang.

Jimmy was sitting on the edge of the bed, looking at the article. "Maybe we should just go with it," he said. "There are worse things to be called than the Old Timers Gang."

"To hell with that," said Emmett. "We're not the Old Timers Gang, goddammit. We're the Emmett Dalton Gang."

"Why does this matter so much to you?" asked Tom, smoking a cigarette.

Emmett felt the blood rushing to his face. "It just does," he said. "I did everything I was supposed to do. I'm supposed to be a legend now. People are supposed to know my name."

"Oh, they know your name," said Jimmy. "They think of you as the leader of the Old Timers Gang, the guy who forgot to put the bullets in his gun—the guy who got locked inside a vault."

"I don't wanna think about that right now," said Emmett.

Jimmy gave him an unhappy look. "Neither do I."

"What are you saying?"

Jimmy shrugged. "It's a little bit embarrassing."

Emmett was getting heated. "What? You don't think I'm cut out to be the leader of this gang?"

"I never said that," said Jimmy.

"Nah," said Tom. "He didn't say that."

Emmett said, "But you were thinking it."

"God as my witness, I wasn't. I swear."

"Maybe it's you who thinks you ain't cut out for this," observed Tom.

Emmett could feel himself becoming more and more angry by the second. He was embarrassed, and as a proud man, this made him feel even more angry. Unsure what to say, Emmett stormed out of the room and went back downstairs to the lobby.

I'm cut out to be the leader, he thought. *I'm the one that put this damn gang together.*

"The man's got issues," said Tom. "I'm not sure he's cut out for this."

Jimmy didn't want to talk about it. "I think he's fine. He's just a little rusty is all."

"A little rusty?" asked Tom, laughing now. "A little rusty don't explain robbin' that bank without any bullets. Bein' rusty don't explain rushing into a robbery without any planning whatsoever. And what about the vault thing? It's more than that. These mistakes he's makin' are big goddamn mistakes. Back in the day, those mistakes woulda got the man shot."

Jimmy looked at him. "What are you saying? You think we should shoot him?"

"Hell no," said Tom. "Shit, I'm too old for that. I'd rather just relax and not shoot anybody."

"So, you think we should just go along with him?"

"How bad do you wanna be a bank robber?"

Jimmy said, "Real bad."

Tom tried to blow a smoke ring but messed it up and it dissipated. Then he turned back to Jimmy and said, "I guess we go along to get along. We let Emmett be the boss and hope to hell he don't get us locked up in the damn hoosegow or worse."

Jimmy looked down at the newspaper again, thinking that the Old Timers Gang wasn't really so bad a name after all.

EMMETT and the boys were packing to leave the Drake when someone knocked at the door. Jimmy walked over to the door, his Peacemaker out, ready for the cops if it was them. He opened the door. There were three Italians standing there, all wearing gaudy suits. Jimmy knew at once they were gangsters.

"How can I help you?" asked Jimmy.

The short, fat one, obviously the leader, said, "You can start by letting us in."

It was at this moment Jimmy noticed one of the men was holding a gun, trained on him.

"And if I say no?" asked Jimmy.

"You won't like what happens next," the man said. "Let us in and everybody gets to walk out of here alive."

Tom spoke up from behind Jimmy. "Let the bastards in."

Jimmy lowered the Peacemaker and moved out of the way so the three men could enter.

"We need you to come with us," said the wop.

"Where we goin'?" asked Emmett.

The goon with the pistol held it up. "Does it matter?"

"I guess not," said Emmett. "Not when you put it like that."

Jimmy started to pick up the suitcase, but the man said, "Leave the suitcase."

"Why?"

The wop grinned. "'Cause I said so. That a good enough reason for you?"

Jimmy shrugged.

"Now, we're all gonna take a walk down the stairs," said the wop, looking at Tom. "At least all of us that can walk. How the hell do you guys get him down there with his wheelchair?"

"There's an elevator," said Emmett.

"Ah," said the wop. "Okay, we're all gonna take the elevator and go downstairs. Then we're taking you to see the boss."

"Who's the boss?" asked Emmett.

"If you can't figure out who we are by now, then maybe you're as dumb as they say in the newspapers," said the man, sneering.

Emmett felt embarrassed and infuriated, but he kept his mouth shut.

The six men went to the elevator, got on, and rode it down to the first floor. They then left the hotel and walked to two black Model As. Emmett and the boys were instructed to split up, and they accompanied the gangsters. Where the hell they were going was anybody's guess. Nobody spoke in either vehicle, so there weren't a lot of clues.

FINALLY, the vehicles stopped, one behind the other, outside a place called the Metropole Hotel on Michigan Street.

As they were getting out of the automobiles, Emmett asked, "This is where your boss is?"

The wop just muttered, "Shut your mouth and do as I say."

Once everyone was out of the Model As, the wop commanded them to walk. They went through the lobby, where no one so much as glanced at them walking with a pistol out and got on the elevator. When they got to the top, they walked to a closed office door with a man standing outside.

"Hey Louie," said the wop. "We're here to see the boss."

Louie, a great big fella that looked like Jack Dempsey, nodded, and opened the door for them. He then stood there in the door frame, taking up half of it, and none of the boys could see who was waiting inside. Just before entering, Tom had a strange thought—he wished Al Capone hadn't gotten shipped off to prison for tax evasion two years before because, as Tom thought, if they had to die, at least they could have met Al Capone first.

When they entered the office, which looked as nondescript as any office ever did, there was a man with big, broad shoulders sitting behind a desk, smoking a cigarette. To his left was another guy, who looked a little too intelligent to be just another dumb goon.

The man behind the desk stood and walked around it with his hand out for Emmett to shake. "Hello, Mr. Dalton."

"Hello," said Emmett, shaking his hand.

"Have a seat," the man directed. "My name is Frank Nitti." He then turned to the man on his left. "And this is my associate, Paul Ricca."

"Why are we here?"

Nitti smiled, and waved at the seats. "Like I said, have a seat, fellas."

Nitti sat at back down at the desk now, his hands folded in front of him, staring at them with a big smile on his face. "The way I see it, you owe me \$20,376 plus the vig."

Emmett sat forward in his seat. "Why's that?"

"Because that's how much you stole from me."

"At the bank?" asked Jimmy.

"At the bank," said Nitti.

Emmett said, "We got $20,376? Hell, we hadn't even counted it yet."

Nitti just kept smiling. "If you know who I am, or know who we are, then you'll understand why this is a predicament. When people steal from us, examples have to be made."

Emmett and Jimmy looked at each other.

"We had no idea that was your money in that bank," said Emmett. "Honest."

Nitti asked, "How would you have?"

"No way we could have."

"Occupational hazard, I guess," said Nitti.

Now Tom spoke up, jonesing from not having had a smoke in twenty minutes. "So, what the hell is it you want?"

"Just the money," said Nitti.

"We don't have it here," said Emmett. "It's back at the hotel."

"We already have the money."

Jimmy asked, "You do?"

"Yes, Mr. McDaniels, we do," said Nitti. "It was in your car, which I might add is an awfully stupid place to leave that much money."

Emmett had a thought. "How much did you take?"

"All of it," said Nitti. "Every last dime."

"What?" asked Emmett. *"You took all our money?"*

"As I said, Mr. Dalton, the $20,376 was the amount you owed us."

"And the rest?" asked Tom.

Nitti grinned big. "Let's call it a little something extra."

Emmett asked, "For what?"

"For not killing you fellas right here," Nitti said dryly.

Now Nitti's partner, Paul Ricca, spoke up. "Remember,

you stole from the Syndicate. You got any idea how many men have died for doing the same? We're giving you the opportunity to walk away from here in one piece."

"Without our money?" asked Tom.

"Why would you allow us to live?" asked Emmett.

Nitti said, "Out of respect. You boys have been in the game for a long time, and we respect that, so we're gonna let you live."

Tom said, "Fuck you, Mr. Nitti," and spit on the floor.

The smiles fell away from Nitti and Ricca's faces.

Ricca pointed at Tom and turned to Emmett. "You better control the old man."

"Or else what?" demanded Tom.

Now Ricca sat forward, opening his jacket to reveal a pistol. "Or else you all get dead. What do you think of that?"

"I think you're nothing but a two-bit hood all dressed up in your father's fancy clothes," said Tom.

Ricca didn't say a word.

Nitti said, "I think we'd better end this meeting now so Mr. Pickett doesn't say something he might regret."

"So that's it?" asked Emmett.

"Pretty much," said Nitti, smiling again.

Emmett asked, "So you just brought us here to tell us you took our money?"

"I brought you here to tell you I wasn't gonna kill you," said Nitti, reaching into his jacket pocket. He then produced a leather wallet. He reached into the wallet and took out a twenty-dollar bill, tossing it on the desk.

"This should pay for a cab to take you boys back to your hotel," said Nitti. "Now do us both a favor and get the fuck out of here before I murder your old asses."

ELEVEN
BULLETS AND PRAYERS

A FEW MONTHS PASSED BY, and Emmett and the boys became better robbers. The rust started to chip away, and they finally managed to get their shit together. But the thing that Emmett was most proud of was that he hadn't shot anybody since St. Louis. He'd winged a fella in Wichita Falls, but that was it. Things had gotten better with Jimmy and Tom, too. Their last six or seven robberies had gone off without a hitch, and nobody questioned Emmett's abilities any longer.

Jimmy had purchased himself a Stetson fedora, and Tom had gotten closer to "the Lord almighty, Jesus fucking Christ." Emmett had called home and learned that Julia was divorcing him on account of his robbing and killing people.

With both Jimmy and Tom alone and sick, and Emmett without a wife, none of them had anything else to live for but robbing banks. It was what they did, and it was who they were. Emmett had been an author and an actor; Jimmy had been a real estate agent; Tom had been a lawman. But today, they were all no-good bank robbers, and they loved every minute of it.

After Melvin Purvis had announced their inclusion onto

the FBI's top ten most wanted list, the media had stopped making fun of them. No one called them the Old Timers Gang anymore, and nobody ever mentioned the mistakes Emmett had made when he'd first returned to the life.

All in all, things were good.

THE EMMETT DALTON Gang was about to rob the Federal Reserve Bank in Kansas City, Missouri. Here they were, in a stolen Ford coupe (they had to change vehicles as they weren't sure they could go on using Emmett's automobile, even with fake tags), brandishing several guns apiece, preparing to rob the place.

Again, they sat idly on the curb in front of the bank, saying a group prayer. The bank would be opening in ten minutes, and they wanted to hit it right off the bat, bright and early.

"Dear God, we are your humble servants," lead Tom, drawing on his cigarette. "We love you and will obey you. Sure, we rob banks, but we try not to hurt anybody when we're doin' it. Hell, God, we haven't shot anybody in months now. So please watch over us, be with us, and be in us, as we prepare to rob these miserable sons of bitches of all their money. We know this is your will that the rich people lose their cash. So it is written, so it shall be done..."

And so on.

AT THAT EXACT SAME MOMENT, a fleet of cars containing members of the Federal Bureau of Investigations was heading towards the bank. Melvin Purvis was in the lead car, a Pierce-Arrow Silver Arrow, along with his right-hand man, Redd White.

"Let us say a little prayer before we go and catch these

robbers," said Melvin. He and Redd both closed their eyes in prayer; Davis Demont did not, as he was driving through Kansas City traffic. "Dear Lord, our father who art in heaven," said Melvin, "We ask that you be with us as we chase these bad men. We ask that you protect us, as we are your humble servants. Dear Lord, we ask that this lead we are following be one that is right and correct, and that we are able to apprehend these robbers with very little bloodshed today..."

And so forth.

As was the norm, Emmett was out front, with his .44-40 caliber Colt single-action revolver out and in the air. Today he was also carrying a .10-gauge shotgun in his other hand; he couldn't say why exactly, but his gut told him to bring it along, so he had. There were only a few customers in the place, as the bank had only just opened its doors a couple minutes before.

Emmett rushed through the bank towards the counter, his gun up, saying, "This here is a robbery. Anyone who doesn't wanna die today better lie down on the floor now and keep his or her hands where I can see 'em." As everyone started moving towards the floor, Emmett motioned to a blonde-haired bank teller with the shotgun. "Not you, honey. I need you to get out a couple of bank bags and fill 'em up with all the cash in these here drawers."

He looked back at Jimmy, who was doing just fine back by the door, his shotgun to the head of the security guard.

So far so good.

Melvin, Redd, and Davis pulled up in front of the bank. Melvin stepped out of the automobile, putting on his trademark white gloves. Redd prepared his Tommy gun—checked it, made sure it was loaded properly—and placed the weapon into his boss' gloved hands.

The other cars were now pulling up behind theirs. Melvin walked towards the FBI officers, all armed to the teeth, now getting out of their vehicles. He motioned for them to take different locations on the street in preparation for the bank robbers' emergence from the bank.

TOM WAS SWEATING LIKE A MOTHERFUCKER. He was only a car's length ahead of that goddamn Melvin Purvis, and he could see him back there, directing his men to take their positions around the bank.

Dear Lord, thought Tom, *please forgive me for what I am about to do.*

He then switched gears, shifting out of park, used the two-by-four to accelerate slowly, and moved out into the street. As he drove off, he could see Purvis and his men scattering in every direction. No one paid him any mind whatsoever.

EMMETT HAD THE BANK MANAGER, a Mr. Carter, up against the wall next to the vault, his revolver in his mouth. "So help me God," Emmett said, "I will shoot you deader than Garfield if you don't open this motherfucking vault and get me my money."

Mr. Carter had no idea how close he was getting to becoming a bloody brain stain on the wall.

Emmett heard a piercing gunshot behind him. He swiveled, his revolver still in Mr. Carter's mouth. He now saw that a customer had tried to rush Jimmy, and Jimmy had been forced to shoot him down.

Fuck it.

These things happen.

Streaks were meant to be broken.

As Emmett was in motion, turning back towards Mr. Carter, a man stood up on the other side of the counter, a pistol in his hand, and fired. The bullet struck Emmett in his right shoulder. The shock from the bullet's impact caused Emmett to squeeze the trigger, making him shoot the bank manager. Mr. Carter started to slide down the wall, leaving a streak of blood and brains as he did. Now there came a third shot from behind Emmett. He spun just in time to see Jimmy blasting the man who had shot Emmett. The man flew back and bounced off the counter, falling out of Emmett's line of sight.

Now what?

With the bank manager dead, their chances of getting into that vault were slim to none. Emmett walked briskly back towards the blonde woman, sacking the cash from the drawers. "Who else knows the combination to that vault?" asked Emmett.

"No one," said the woman. "Honest."

Emmett raised his bloody pistol in her direction.

"I swear!" she yelled out.

He squeezed the trigger, and the woman went flying back against the counter, inadvertently flinging the money into the air as she fell.

"Let's get the fuck out of here!" yelled Jimmy.

When Melvin Purvis heard the shots inside, he knew his tip had been a solid one. He was still standing by the automobile, having not yet found a place to hide when he saw the two robbers—Dalton and McDaniels—come running out of the bank. With no proper place to hide, Melvin was forced to crouch down between vehicles just ahead of them.

. . .

EMMETT DIDN'T UNDERSTAND.

"Where the fuck is Tom?" he screamed.

Jimmy was the first one to notice the FBI men scattered all around them, beginning to move out of their hiding places. *"The goddamn FBI!"* he shouted. He raised his shotgun in the direction of a cluster of them and was immediately shot down.

MELVIN STEPPED out from between the parked cars now. He wanted to be the one who took out Emmett Dalton. Again, this wasn't about Melvin's ego; it was about doing the finest job he could possibly do. He started moving towards Dalton, who didn't yet see him.

And then Dalton did the unthinkable. He dodged the bullets flying at him from across the road and jumped into a moving automobile on the passenger side. Melvin started to run now, trying to catch up to him, but it was no use.

Emmett Dalton went speeding past him.

"PLEASE DON'T HURT ME, MISTER," said the man driving the automobile.

To this, Emmett said, "Open up your door and jump out or else you die." To his credit, the man didn't hesitate. He just swung the door open and jumped out of the moving vehicle, falling hard to the pavement.

Emmett scooted over and took the wheel, stomping on the accelerator as he did. He looked back in the mirror and saw nothing.

TWELVE
FACE OFF

After Emmett Dalton had raced past him in a hijacked Ford, Melvin Purvis had jumped back into his own vehicle, with Redd now driving. Melvin was clinging to the Tommy gun tightly now, and his teeth were chattering. He wasn't afraid —no, he was *excited* now, perhaps the most excited he'd ever been.

They drove for a moment, gaining speed, before they saw the stolen automobile ahead, swerving in and out of traffic.

"I'm gonna try and take him here," said Melvin.

Redd turned to him. "*Here?* It's awfully goddamn busy here, boss."

"Maybe, but it all stops today."

Emmett was weaving in and out of traffic, pushing the automobile up to its max at sixty-five miles per hour. He almost got nailed by oncoming traffic several times, but always managed to find his way back into his own lane at just the right moment to avoid collision.

He looked back in his rear-view mirror now, and he saw them. The bastards were back there. Of course, it was still a hell of a distance, but he swore it looked like Melvin Purvis himself there in the Silver Arrow. But what the hell was he doing? He could see clearly that the man was now hanging himself out the passenger side window.

THE WIND WAS in Melvin's face. He had to squint to see, but he could still make out that bastard Emmett Dalton up there ahead of them.

"Speed up," he ordered to Redd.

Redd said, "I'm going as fast as I can. This sucker won't go any faster!"

Now Melvin saw Emmett slow down for a moment to avoid a collision. Melvin raised the barrel of the Tommy gun, aiming it towards the stolen car, and he squeezed the trigger.

EMMETT FIGURED out what the hell Purvis was doing just a millisecond before the federal agent opened fire on him. A hail of bullets struck the Ford, but none of them touched Emmett. Stunned and confused, he swerved the vehicle, scraping up against an oncoming automobile on his left.

Emmett had to think fast now. He made himself focus. Once he had his bearings about him again, he pulled the steering wheel hard to the right. The Ford jumped up over the curb, scraping its side along several store fronts. Emmett very nearly struck a woman walking on the sidewalk, but luckily, she dove out of the way at the very last second.

Emmett couldn't see shit from where he was.

He stomped the brake and slid the thing into park.

He jumped out of the car, the Colt in his right hand, the

shotgun in his left. Seeing the entrance to a diner only a couple feet away, he jumped from the vehicle and ran towards it.

WHAT THE HELL was Emmett Dalton doing? Melvin watched him swerve to the right and jump up over the curb. At first, he thought he'd hit him, but then the Ford ground to a halt up ahead. Melvin squeezed the trigger again, and the Tommy gun sprayed bullets all over the automobile. Much to Melvin's chagrin, he didn't hit Dalton. Just before the spray of bullets reached the left side where Dalton had been, the robber leaped from the vehicle into a store.

As Redd and Melvin approached, Melvin could see now that it was a diner.

The cocksucker was in there.

"*Stop here!*" ordered Melvin.

He could hear screams from inside the diner.

NO ONE in the diner knew how to react when they saw the commotion followed by Emmett's barreling in, carrying the two guns. Someone screamed, and several others dove onto the floor. A few people stood and ran towards the entrance.

Emmett reached out and snatched a heavyset woman trying to run past him. He put the Colt to her head and said, "Don't try anything funny. I'll shoot."

WHEN MELVIN GOT to the entrance of the diner, a smattering of people came running out past him. Through the crowd he could just make out Emmett Dalton moving back towards the back of the place with a woman in his arms.

Melvin turned to Redd. "You ready?"

"Sure thing, boss," said Redd.

Melvin led the way, walking calmly past people running, the Tommy gun out in front of him. He could now see Emmett Dalton clearly. He had a Colt revolver up to a woman's head.

Melvin kept moving towards him, slowly and confidently.

Dalton was backed into a corner. Right then and there Melvin decided that the hostage could live or die, but he was killing or apprehending Emmett Dalton today, no matter what.

Dalton panicked, readjusting the Colt so Melvin could see it clearly. "Try any shit and this woman dies," said Dalton.

"Let's you and I have a talk," said Melvin.

Dalton didn't know how to react to this. *"What the hell?"* he said.

"We're just gonna talk this thing out."

Dalton's eyes narrowed to slits, and he looked at Melvin, trying to figure out what the hell was happening.

"My name is Melvin Purvis."

"I know," said Dalton. "I saw you in the newspapers."

"And I see your picture plastered all over my office walls," said Melvin.

Dalton readjusted the pistol again. "I'm telling you—I'll shoot this broad."

Melvin smiled. "I believe you, Mr. Dalton."

"If you want this woman to live, you gotta let me outta here."

"That's never gonna happen."

The woman's eyes got big, and she looked even more terrified now than she had before.

"This man to my right has the unfortunate name of Redd White," said Melvin.

Dalton looked at Redd, aiming a rifle at him.

"Old Redd here is a sharpshooter. If I tell him to take you out, he's gonna take you out. Do you understand?"

"Fuck you," managed Dalton.

At that moment, the hostage elbowed Dalton in the ribs and managed to break free. Before Dalton could react, both Melvin and Redd shot him. Caught in the hail of sub-machine gun bullets, Emmett Dalton's body danced rhythmically for a moment before finally falling to the ground.

And Emmett Dalton was no more.

THIRTEEN
CONCLUSION

AFTER CONCLUDING his speech about the deaths of Emmett Dalton and Jimmy McDaniels, Melvin Purvis took questions from the reporters who filled the room. "How many members of the Emmett Dalton Gang are still at large?" asked one.

Melvin said, "We're not sure. There may be one man still out there, there may be two. We have no knowledge at this time as to who the other members of Emmett Dalton's gang were."

TOM PICKETT HAD a hell of a time transferring himself out of the automobile into his wheelchair without assistance. It took over an hour, but finally he was back in his wheelchair, strapped in and safe.

He'd parked a block away so no one would see the stolen automobile. It took all the strength he had, but he managed to wheel himself around the block, smoking one last cigarette as he did.

As he wheeled himself up towards the entrance to Sunnyvale Rest Home, he saw a familiar face approaching. It was

Charlene, one of the nurses who worked there. "Tom Pickett, where in the blazes have you been?" she asked. "We been worried sick about you. We thought you was kidnapped."

Pretending to have dementia, Tom feigned ignorance. "Do I know you?"

And this is how Tom Pickett lived to be seventy-eight years old.

Dear reader,

We hope you enjoyed reading *Six-Guns Blazing*. Please take a moment to leave a review, even if it's a short one. Your opinion is important to us.

Discover more books by Andy Rausch at
https://www.nextchapter.pub/authors/andy-rausch

Want to know when one of our books is free or discounted?
Join the newsletter at http://eepurl.com/bqqB3H

Best regards,
Andy Rausch and the Next Chapter Team

Six-Guns Blazing
ISBN: 978-4-82410-056-6

Published by
Next Chapter
1-60-20 Minami-Otsuka
170-0005 Toshima-Ku, Tokyo
+818035793528

24th August 2021